THE UNSUNG HERO

BY
ALISON ROBERTS

MILLS & BOON

First published in Great Britain 2011
by Mills & Boon, an imprint of Harlequin (UK) Limited.
Large Print edition 2011
Harlequin (UK) Limited, Eton House,
18-24 Paradise Road, Richmond, Surrey TW9 1SR

© Alison Roberts 2011

ISBN: 978 0 263 21767 4

Harlequin (UK) policy is to use papers that are natural, renewable and recyclable products and made from wood grown in sustainable forests. The logging and manufacturing process conform to the legal environmental regulations of the country of origin.

Printed and bound in Great Britain
by CPI Antony Rowe, Chippenham, Wiltshire

THE HEART OF A REBEL

Legendary doctors
who aren't afraid to break the rules!

Mills & Boon® Medical™ Romance brings you a brand-new trilogy from favourite author Alison Roberts!

There'd been four of them once upon a time. But, after the loss of their best friend, now there is just Max, Rick and Jet. These rebel doctors have formed an unbreakable brotherhood—a bond that would see them put their lives on the line for each other…

Now these bad boys are about to be tamed!
But it'll take a special kind of woman
to see past their tough exteriors
and find the heart of a rebel…

This month meet Max
(THE HONOURABLE MAVERICK)
and Rick (THE UNSUNG HERO).

Then look out for Jet's story, coming soon!

The Heart of a Rebel

Legendary doctors
who aren't afraid to break the rules!

Dear Reader

OK. Personal confession time, here :-)

I'm one of those women who find certain tough, leather-clad men who ride powerful motorbikes irresistibly sexy.

Can this image be improved on?

I thought so. What if these men are also fabulously good-looking, highly intelligent, and capable of putting their lives on the line for the people they love?

For each other.

For children.

For their women.

These are my 'bad boys'. Max, Rick and Jet. Bonded by a shared tragedy in the past, but not barred from a future filled with love.

Enjoy.

I certainly did :-)

With love

Alison

Alison Roberts lives in Christchurch, New Zealand. She began her working career as a primary school teacher, but now juggles available working hours between writing and active duty as an ambulance officer. Throwing in a large dose of parenting, housework, gardening and pet-minding keeps life busy, and teenage daughter Becky is responsible for an increasing number of days spent on equestrian pursuits. Finding time for everything can be a challenge, but the rewards make the effort more than worthwhile.

Recent titles by the same author:

ST PIRAN'S: THE BROODING
   HEART SURGEON†
THE MARRY-ME WISH*
WISHING FOR A MIRACLE*
NURSE, NANNY…BRIDE!
HOT-SHOT SURGEON, CINDERELLA BRIDE
THE ITALIAN SURGEON'S
   CHRISTMAS MIRACLE

†*St Piran's Hospital*
*Part of the *Baby Gift* collection

CHAPTER ONE

TIME stood still.

Rick Wilson had never actually understood that phrase before this moment but, man, he did now.

It was kind of like one of those three-hundred-and-sixty-degree shots in a movie where something was frozen in space but the rest of the scene continued around it. He was part of that scene but where he was and what he was here for became suddenly and completely irrelevant.

It seemed extraordinary that nobody else had noticed but why would they? The only thing that had really stopped was in his head. A stun-gun effect on his thought processes from that first sight of…perfection, that was the only word for it.

Some kind of goddess in a floaty blue dress.

Long, long blonde hair, some of which had been wound around her head and adorned with tiny, white flowers. She was tall and slim and he'd put good money on her eyes being blue. Dark blue.

Who was she and where the hell had she been? Nowhere near his world, that was for sure, because he would have remembered.

More than his brain had been stunned but it wasn't until the need for oxygen made Rick suck in a rather deep breath that he realised his chest had also been immobilised. The sound he made elicited a nudge from the man standing close by his side. And a look. He might as well have had a bubble over his head like a cartoon character as well. One that said, *Do me a favour and try and keep your hands off her for the duration of the ceremony at least.*

No worries. Rick's grin flashed back. How long could a ceremony last, after all?

Suddenly, the annoyance of wearing the ridiculous bow-tie and the vaguely trapped feeling that weddings in general, and this one in particular, always gave him became worthwhile. He was actually pleased he was dressed up to the nines. That he would be here for hours and that one of his official duties was to partner the bridesmaid. The goddess, no less.

She was much closer now. With a supreme effort, Rick tried to stop staring. He managed to switch off the mental zoom lens and take in some of the wider picture. He could hear the music and see the way the small gathering of guests in this garden setting had twisted in their seats to watch the bride and her bridesmaid approaching. A small boy was in front of the two women, throwing handfuls of rose petals from the basket he was carrying.

The sight of the child triggered a process of recalling snatches of conversations he now wished he'd paid more attention to. Worry over the choice of a bridesmaid because…that's right, she had a kid who was very sick. Only it wasn't her kid, exactly. He was a nephew or something but she was his only family and she was clearly some sort of saint because she'd been travelling the globe trying to track down his biological father so that the kid's leukaemia could be treated with a bone-marrow transplant.

What was her name?

Rick was thinking hard as he watched the boy being directed to sit in an empty seat in the front row.

Sarah.

That was it. Nice name.

He had to wait while the bridesmaid positioned herself beside the bride and took charge of the bouquet but, finally, she looked up and caught his welcoming smile. Her eyes widened a fraction and she held the eye contact for a heartbeat longer. Then she looked away as the celebrant began to speak and welcome those gathered to witness the ceremony. It took Rick a few seconds to realise why he was feeling oddly poleaxed again.

She hadn't smiled back, that was why.

Sarah had to take a deep, deep breath.

It was good that she had the bouquet to hold because it effectively hid the slight tremor she could feel in her hands. She hadn't expected him to look at her like that—as though he couldn't wait to launch a campaign to jump her bones. A stupid oversight, really, because she ought to be used to that kind of reaction from men by now. It was just so wildly inappropriate at this moment that she had an insane urge to slap his face. So she held on to that bunch of flowers for dear life and listened to the familiar words of a traditional wedding ceremony.

'I, Maxwell McAdam, take thee, Eleanor Peters, to be my wife. To have and to hold...'

Maybe she'd misinterpreted the look. He was probably just a nice guy, as Ellie had assured her he was. He was the best man and it was his job to look after the bridesmaid, wasn't it? To be friendly.

'To love and cherish from this day forward. This is my solemn vow.'

Sarah found her gaze drifting sideways in the tiny pause as the bride, her friend Ellie, prepared to take her turn to recite the vows. If Rick was doing his job properly, he'd be focused on the ceremony. Thinking about the rings he would need to produce very soon. To her consternation, however, she found herself catching his direct gaze again. How long had he been looking at *her*?

At least he was looking suitably serious this time, with no hint of that confident, playboy smile but there was a question in those dark eyes that had nothing to do with what they were a part of at this moment and if she simply turned away it would be a rebuff that could have repercussions.

Enormous repercussions.

Her tiny smile might have been hesitant but it was enough for that unspoken question to vanish. For Rick's face to soften a fraction in that split second before they both looked away.

'I, Eleanor Peters, take thee, Maxwell McAdam, to be my husband. To have and to hold…'

The first kiss as husband and wife was a moment that would be etched on Rick's brain for ever. The way Max and Ellie looked at each other.

The soft intensity in the way their lips touched to seal their commitment. The way the kiss went on…and on.

Impossible not to feel the power of the link between this newly married couple and it was strong enough to give Rick an odd twisting sensation in his gut. A combination of recognition and…loss?

Recognition was automatic. He'd known Max since high school. Since, along with Jet and Matt, they'd formed a brotherhood that had become true family for all of them. Labelled the 'bad boys', they'd had the kind of bond that meant you'd put your life on the line for them in a heartbeat and life without the strength and power of that support crew was unimaginable.

Loss came from the uneasy feeling that the order of his universe was changing because one of the 'bad boys' was no longer a single entity. He had a ready-made family, in fact, what with Ellie's baby Mattie. Fast bike rides and nights out with fabulous women were a thing of the past. Max was now committed to sharing his life with a woman and the bond between them was clearly cemented with the same kind of soul-deep glue that Rick had only known with the brotherhood.

Was it really possible to feel that way about a *woman*?

The guests were clapping and cheering. A whistle or two could be heard. Rick glanced sideways to where Jet was seated in the front row. The third 'bad boy' had been given the responsibility of caring for baby Mattie during the ceremony and he was still holding her with the kind of expression that made Rick think of a bomb-disposal expert in the middle of a dangerous mission. A focused scowl that suggested appreciation of both the significance of the mission and its less-than-desirable potential.

Noticing the direction of Rick's gaze, Jet rolled his eyes as the kiss finally wound up. It took him back to the conversation they'd had only last night, over a few beers. To them both vowing to avoid the kind of commitment Max had chosen. They'd keep their bikes, thanks very much. They'd work hard and play hard and take all the fun life had to offer because they knew damn well how short it could be.

The boy beside Jet was making a disgusted face but then he grinned repentantly at Sarah, who had also looked away from the couple. It was inevitable that their gazes brushed as they turned back to their duties. With the image of that kiss still burning itself into Rick's memory cells, along with the reminder of that vow to play hard and get the most out of life, it was just as inevitable that his gaze dropped from Sarah's eyes to her mouth.

Such a soft-looking, deliciously kissable kind of mouth.

He felt his breath leave his lungs in a soft sigh as he wondered...

No, make that anticipated. And, knowing he could trust that very pleasant curl in his gut, he knew that kissing Sarah was something he had very good reason to look forward to. All he needed now was a smooth opening line and that shouldn't be a problem given the amount of practice he'd had over the last decade or more.

First, there were the congratulations to be given to the newly married couple. Rick thumped Max on the back to accentuate his hug and then kissed Ellie, whose eyes were shining with joyous tears.

'Thanks, Rick.' She turned from him to receive Sarah's hug. ''Bout time we introduced you two,' she said. 'Rick, this is—'

'Sarah,' he cut in, smiling. 'I've heard all about you.'

She looked disconcerted, turning back to Ellie, but the bride was being taken to a small table on one side of the flower-covered gazebo to deal with the paperwork.

'W-what have you heard?'

'You're an old friend of Ellie's.'

'We were flatmates in Auckland.'

'And didn't you sublet your apartment here to Max?'

'Yes. I was away in the States for a while.'

Rick nodded. 'So, really, you're responsible for this wedding happening. If Ellie hadn't come looking for you, she would never have met Max.'

And *he* would never have met Sarah. Now,

that could have been a smooth opening gambit except that he didn't have time to deliver it. The signatures of the witnesses were now required and both Rick and Sarah had duties to perform. After that, group photographs were taken with the lovely backdrop of this garden that Max and Ellie's new property boasted, the photographer's attention focused on the bride and groom. Rick had more time to think but, annoyingly, inspiration wouldn't strike.

Maybe that had something to do with the munchkins. Mattie was back in her mother's arms now, much to Jet's obvious relief, and the boy was glued to Sarah's side as they watched some family shots being taken. Ellie held Mattie and Max held Ellie and nobody who saw those photographs in years to come would ever guess that Max wasn't Mattie's biological father.

It didn't even seem that crazy any more, though Rick certainly couldn't see himself putting his hand up to adopt an infant. He took another glance at the boy standing beside Sarah. Weird that her living accessory wasn't the deal-breaker it would have been even a few months ago but this was a kid, not a baby, and, anyway, he was a special enough case to make allowances for.

'Let's get a photo of all the boys in their suits,' Ellie suggested. 'Josh, come and stand with Max and Rick.'

'Do I *have* to?'

'Yes.' Sarah gave him a stern look but then smiled winningly. 'Please? For me? And Ellie?'

Oh, man… That was a real smile. One that no man could possibly resist. Even a half-grown one.

'All right. I s'pose,' Josh grumbled.

He was soon standing between the groom and the best man, a miniature version of the two tall men in his small suit and bow-tie. He had dark hair, too. What was left of it. Rick could see the pale skin of the boy's scalp and knew it wouldn't be long before he was completely bald. He could also see that Sarah was watching him watch Josh and she had an odd look on her face.

Did she know that he knew the history? Was she worried that it might colour the way he talked to the boy? She needn't worry. Rick dealt with a lot of seriously ill children and he wasn't about to talk down to the lad or exude sympathy. The smile he gave Sarah was intended to reassure her but, strangely, she looked distinctly uncomfortable.

If it hadn't been too weird a thought to entertain, he might have even interpreted her expression as vaguely guilty.

Did she think he was directing sympathy at her, maybe? As if. He had enough sensitivity to know that she wouldn't appreciate that. She was clearly a strong and capable woman. Someone who'd taken on the responsibility of a child who wasn't her own. Who was having to cope with the disaster of that child becoming gravely ill and who was doing everything she possibly could to put things right.

He respected that. Good grief, she'd gone to the other side of the world to try and track down the boy's dad and when she'd discovered he wasn't the one, she'd headed back to chase up another lead. Hopefully, that had proved successful.

What with all the drama of Max and Ellie in recent months and then getting them shifted to this house and the wedding being planned, Rick hadn't caught up on any further news about that. He had heard that Josh had been in hospital again in Auckland, which was why Sarah had only just made it to Dunedin in time to be Ellie's bridesmaid. Maybe that had been for the transplant.

'Hey, buddy.' He winked at Josh as they positioned themselves near an old sundial in a corner of the garden. 'How's it going?'

Josh eyed him warily.

'I'm Rick.'

'I know. You're Max's friend.'

'Yep.' Both men spoke together and then Max put his arm over Josh's shoulders as cameras whirred. 'Rick's got a Ducati too. Just like mine.' He raised an eyebrow at Rick. 'Josh was looking at that photo of us last night. With the bikes.'

'Max said he might give me a ride one day.'

'Cool.' Rick had no trouble smiling for the camera. Maybe this was it. His ticket for getting to know Sarah. Max was going to be very busy settling into married life. *He* could offer to give Josh that ride.

'I don't think so.'

Sarah held out her hand to accept the glass of juice she had requested at the drinks table, congratulating herself on being so restrained.

Had Rick been waiting for a moment when she was away from everybody else to make his unwelcome offer to give Josh a ride on his motorbike?

Over my dead body had been the words that first sprang to mind but she had managed—with difficulty—to stop them emerging. She didn't want to antagonise this man. OK, maybe this *was* a long shot but it was the only shot she had left and she couldn't afford to throw it away. And maybe she should have been as prepared for something like this as for the way Rick was making no secret of finding her attractive.

He was totally irresponsible. The kind of good-looking—well, OK, make that *great*-looking guy who skated through life getting everything he wanted and to hell with any less than pleasant consequences. How old was he? Thirty-five or -six? High time he woke up and smelled the coffee, that's for sure, but what was she going to do if he simply refused?

'I'm not suggesting anything remotely dangerous.' Rick pulled a can of lager from the nest of ice in a big silver tub. 'Just a slow crawl around the block, or something.'

The smile revealed that Rick Wilson usually got what he wanted and no wonder. It was a winning smile, for sure. Confident and lazy. Softening a face of definite lines and a shadowed jaw that had 'bad boy' stamped all over it. Soft, dark hair that had been neatly combed into place a while back but the breeze in this outdoor setting had detached a single lock that almost touched an equally dark eyebrow. Eyes that had a hint of mischief that any woman would have trouble resisting.

Any other woman, that was.

'I don't think so,' Sarah repeated, trying very hard not to put a punctuation mark between each word. She even added a smile of her own. 'But thanks anyway.'

His smile faded. A tiny frown appeared between his eyes.

Oh…help.

As if in answer to the silent plea, there was a rustle of silk beside her and Ellie reached for one of the cans in the tub of ice.

'For Max.' She grinned in response to Rick's raised eyebrows. 'He's got his hands full of baby at the moment.' Then she looked from Rick to Sarah and she paused, her eyes widening.

Sarah gave her head a tiny shake. No, she hadn't broken her promise.

'Rick was just offering to give Josh a ride on his bike,' she said, her tone carefully neutral.

'Oh…' Ellie bit her lip, giving Rick an oddly sympathetic glance. 'Um…Josh's mother was killed when she was a pillion passenger on her boyfriend's bike,' she said quietly.

Rick winced visibly. 'Sorry.'

'No worries. You weren't to know.' Sarah could

see Josh approaching. 'Here's your juice,' she said brightly. 'Want something to eat as well?'

'Nah. I've already had heaps. Can we go down to the beach? Max says there's a jetty and you can go fishing.'

'Maybe another day. We're here for the wedding, remember? And not for too much longer, either. You don't want to get too tired when you're going to be starting school again this week.'

This wasn't going well.

If it wasn't his wedding day, he might have given Max a bit of stick for setting him up for that little disaster of offering Josh the opportunity to get maimed or worse.

He still could, if he made a joke of it, but there was something even more disturbing that needed his attention urgently.

Sarah was talking to Jet now. Smiling and nodding at something he was saying. Rick broke off the conversation he was having with some theatre nurses he knew and moved in their direction. The clock was ticking here because who knew how long it would be before she whisked Josh off home? And what if she was busy agreeing to a date or something? No. Rick could be pretty sure he was safe on that score. Jet wouldn't go near a woman who had a child. The mere mention of babies had been enough at times for his mate to hold up crossed fingers and make a hissing sound to ward off bad voodoo.

'We'll have to see how it goes,' Sarah was saying as he got close enough to hear. 'One step at a time.'

'Hey…' Jet seemed happy enough to include Rick in the conversation. 'Did you know Sarah's a specialised ICU nurse? She's coming back to work at Queen Mary's next week.'

'Just casual to start with,' Sarah added. 'I'm not sure how it'll go. All depends on Josh, of course.'

'Of course.' Rick gave up trying to find a smooth opening line. Instead, he went for something much more mundane. 'Our paths will be crossing. I spend quite a good percentage of my time in ICU.'

'You're a neurosurgeon, yes?'

'Yes.' This was good. Had she been asking someone about *him*? Even better that she would be working in that department. Given that neurosurgery was often the main specialty involved in cases like head injuries, he often spent considerable periods of time in ICU. But then he frowned.

'Coming back? You've worked there before?' Surely he would have spotted her. In the unit or the cafeteria. Even the car park, dammit. He was absolutely certain he would have noticed.

Sarah's expression was rueful. 'I applied for a job and got it but I never actually did a shift. That was when Josh got diagnosed.'

'ALL?' Jet queried.

Sarah's nod was grim. Acute lymphoblastic leukaemia was the stuff of parental nightmares. 'The next few months were a bit of a blur. All the invasive diagnostic tests and then induction chemotherapy. I lived in the children's oncology unit.'

'Good response to induction?' It was Jet who spoke again.

Sarah shook her head this time. 'Slow enough to be a real concern. We finally achieved remission but that was when I was told he was a candidate for an early HSCT.'

Rick was listening carefully despite being fascinated by watching Sarah's face as she spoke. She was genuine all right. Nuances of emotion played across her features and he could feel the agony she'd been through. God help him, but he had an insane urge to wrap her into his arms and hold her close. He shook it off and focused on what she'd been saying.

HSCT. Haematopoietic stem-cell transplant. More commonly known as a bone-marrow transplant.

'And that took you to the States?' he asked. 'To try and locate a donor?'

Sarah's gaze flicked in his direction. She hesitated before responding but he couldn't read her expression this time. It was almost as if shutters had come down but he could tell she was struggling with *something*. Then she looked away from both her companions, her gaze raking the small crowd now scattered throughout the garden.

Many were holding champagne glasses and some had plates, having helped themselves to a sumptuous afternoon tea from the table laden with silver, tiered stands that held everything from savouries and sandwiches to tiny cupcakes decorated with hearts. Imitating Sarah's observation, Rick spotted Josh, who was sitting on the wide steps of the terrace beside Max, who was feeding Mattie with a bottle.

Of course. She wouldn't want to be discussing this if Josh was within earshot.

'We heard that didn't work out,' he said gently. 'But Auckland was more successful, yes?'

'What?' Those dark blue eyes flashed with… what?…*alarm*? 'What makes you say that?'

Rick sighed inwardly. He was only trying to be interested here. Supportive. Was she always this prickly?

'Ellie mentioned that Josh was in hospital,

ALISON ROBERTS 29

that's all. And that was why there was some doubt about whether you'd make it to the wedding. I knew you'd gone to Auckland because of another donor possibility so I was hoping that was due to a transplant happening.'

'No.' He could see the deep breath Sarah took. 'He got sick. Pneumonia. A bug he probably picked up from the plane trip home.'

She was watching Josh again. Ellie had gone over to the steps and was sitting beside her brand-new husband but leaning forward, talking to Josh on his other side. Then she stood up and began walking towards Rick. He glanced at Jet but there seemed to be nothing to say to break the suddenly tense silence enclosing the three of them.

Josh's condition was fragile. He might or might not still be in remission but even if he was, he was at risk due to his suppressed immune system that the maintenance drug regime would cause. Any bacterial, viral or fungal infection could be potentially fatal. Ellie joined the group but it didn't relieve the tension. If anything, it went up a notch or two even before she spoke.

'Sarah…I'm sorry but Josh isn't feeling very well. He says he's got a headache and he thinks he's going to be sick.'

'Oh, *no*!' Rick saw the colour drain from Sarah's face.

'It could just be too many chocolate éclairs and sunshine but…'

The tiny word hung in the air. It could be an infection of some kind. It could even be a sign of a central nervous system relapse, which would not only take away the status of remission but could escalate the progression of this boy's disease.

'I'll have to get him checked.' Sarah's eyes were bright. Too bright. Glittering with unshed tears? 'Oh, *God*… We've only just got over the last setback. He was so desperate to stay well enough to go to school again.'

'I'm so sorry.' Ellie was biting her bottom lip. 'Jet could take you into Emergency.' She turned. 'You've got a shift starting later tonight, haven't you?'

'Yeah.'

'He knows everyone,' she said to Sarah. 'He'll make sure Josh gets the best of care.'

'I'll go too,' Rick announced.

The others all looked at him in surprise.

'Jet and I came together,' he said quickly. 'In my car. It's not as if you guys are planning formal speeches or anything, are you?' He didn't give Ellie time to respond. 'Jet can look after Josh and everything that needs to happen. I can look after Sarah.'

It felt good to say that. And he meant every word. Smooth opening lines or first kisses were the last thing on his mind right now. This was about a potentially sick kid and the woman who was, effectively, his mother. There was no hidden agenda or ulterior motive.

The 'bad boys' weren't being disbanded by this marriage, he realised in a moment of sudden clarity. The tribe was simply expanding. Ellie was a part of it and, by association, Sarah came under the same protective umbrella. That was what this was about. Solidarity. A tribe thing.

So why did Sarah and Ellie exchange a glance that made him feel as if he'd stepped into a mine-field?

'I think…' Ellie spoke after a loaded pause and her voice sounded strange. 'That might be quite a good idea, don't you, Sarah?'

Equally strangely, Sarah had closed her eyes as though offering up a silent prayer. She opened them slowly, stared at Ellie for a second and then turned her head towards Rick.

The gaze was so intense it rang alarm bells that were positively deafening. What the hell was going on here?

'Yes.' Sarah sounded perfectly calm, which was weird in itself. 'It *is* a good idea. Can we go now, please?'

Josh had been diagnosed with leukaemia here at Queen Mary's and it became rapidly obvious that he was a favourite patient amongst the paediatric oncology staff that got summoned to the emergency department. One of the registrars even called his consultant, Mike Randall, who said he would be coming in to see what was happening.

A lot was happening. Numerous blood tests and a chest X-ray. An exhaustive physical examination, abdominal ultrasound and a lumbar puncture. Jet changed into scrubs and simply went on shift early but Rick was left with little to do but be there and observe, feeling somewhat ridiculous in his dinner suit and the bow-tie, which had come undone but he wasn't about to bother retying it.

Sarah would have probably felt absurdly overdressed, too, in that long frock and with the flowers still in her hair but it didn't seem to occur to her. As pale as her nephew, she was there by his side for every moment. Holding his hand for the blood tests and curled protectively close to his head throughout the lumbar puncture procedure. Rustling in her long dress as she walked beside his bed when it was rolled to a different area. She said little but seemed grateful to have Jet and

Rick there to smooth the admission process and the transition of care to the oncology department.

Josh was just as stoical as Sarah. The hospital environment and these frightening and painful procedures were a part of life for both of them now and they were in it together. With every passing minute, Rick became more aware of the striking bond between these two. Of their courage. Josh didn't cry, even once, and Rick was left convinced that Sarah was a vital component of any treatment for this child. The gentle way she touched him, almost constantly, and the way she held direct eye contact throughout the worst moments, infusing him with both strength and comfort, touched something very deep in Rick.

All his younger patients had families that loved them and would do anything they could to help but he'd never witnessed a bond quite like this. They were both special but Sarah…she was astonishing.

By the time the consultant, Mike, arrived, the early testing was complete and Josh had been moved to a private room in the children's ward. Surprisingly, Max turned up at the same time.

'What are you doing here, man?' Rick asked. 'It's your wedding night!'

'Ellie sent me in with some clothes for Sarah and to find out what's happening. How's Josh?'

'I think we're about to find out.' Rick tilted his head to where Mike was gripping Sarah's hand.

'I hoped it would be an outpatient appointment when we got to see you again,' the older doctor was saying. 'You've only just come down from Auckland, haven't you?'

'Yesterday,' Sarah confirmed wryly.

They both looked at the still figure of the sleeping child on the bed beside them. He had a pulse oximeter on a finger and an IV line snaking up from a heavily bandaged elbow to the stand supporting bags of medicated fluids.

'Let's step outside for a minute so we don't wake him up,' Mike suggested. 'He'll be worn out by now, I suspect.'

He raised his eyebrows as they reached the two men standing by the door. 'Rick...this is a bit out of your field, isn't it? And, Max…didn't I hear you were getting married today?'

'I did. Sarah was our bridesmaid and Josh was the pageboy.'

'Ahh…' Mike's smile was warm. 'And there I was thinking you'd all dressed up on my ac-count.'

He pulled the door almost closed behind him and they drifted closer to the window where they could still see Josh. The ward was quiet ant the corridor dimly lit, with evening visiting hours well over. A baby began crying somewhere and a child's voice called out for her mother. It was a subdued and slightly miserable background.

Mike spoke softly. 'We still haven't got all the results back yet, of course. And I've scheduled a bone-marrow biopsy and MRI scan for tomorrow morning.'

Sarah made a low sound of distress that cut Rick like a sharp blade. Mike's face creased in sympathy.

'I know. I'm sorry. The good news is that his fever's dropped and his lungs are clear. There's no significant change in the size of his liver or spleen and his kidney function's looking good. Even better, this doesn't look like CNS involvement. I think the symptoms are probably due to a virus and we've got treatment under way to deal with it. Antivirals and antibiotics to cover all the bases.'

'He was going to try and go back to school this week. Said he'd wear a mask even if it made him look like a freak.'

Mike shook his head, dismissing the possibility. 'We'll have him in here for a bit. I want to make sure he's still in remission. If not, we're going to have to get back into a pretty aggressive chemotherapy programme.'

Sarah closed her eyes and Rick could sense her struggle in trying to find the strength to face what was coming. He felt helpless.

'What about HSCT?' he asked Mike. 'That's going to be the best option, isn't it?'

Mike's expression was grim. 'No siblings, unfortunately. Sarah's the only family and she's nowhere near a match. Nothing's come up on the bone-marrow register and she hasn't been able to trace Josh's father.' He turned to Sarah. 'You didn't get any further in your hunt in Auckland, did you?'

Her eyes were open now. She was staring at Rick but her gaze flicked back to Mike.

'Actually, I think I did. Quite by chance and only because of Josh being admitted for the chest infection. One of the nurses in the ward had been working there for ages and she seemed to know everybody.'

'And?' There was an undercurrent of excitement in Mike's tone.

'I've got a possibility to chase up. I…I'm just not sure how co-operative he might be.'

'You think he'd refuse to help?' Rick could hear more than a hint of outrage in his own voice.

'He might. He doesn't even know he's got a son yet.'

Rick gave a dismissive snort. 'Tough. It's not as if he's had to take any responsibility so far, is it?'

'No.'

Sarah's agreement was cautious. She was giving him an odd look, as though wondering why he was pushing this, but there was an element of something like hope in her face and that made Rick feel good. Very good. He was helping here.

'But that's not exactly his fault,' she added. 'He didn't know. I don't think Josh's mother even knew.'

'Doesn't matter.' Rick was confident now. He ignored the way Max was staring at him as though he was about to step off a cliff or something. He could support Sarah in this quest. Help her. Maybe help Josh as well. 'If he's a decent human being,' he said firmly, 'then getting tested is the least he can do.'

Sarah looked away from him to Max who gave her a slow nod of encouragement. She looked back at Rick.

'I hope you meant that,' she said softly. 'How soon do you think you could arrange to have the test?'

CHAPTER TWO

'What?'

He was looking at her as if she was some kind of alien species, clearly unable to make any sense of her request. Sarah glanced at Max but he was watching his friend and had an expression of sympathy that made her heart sink. He knew how hard it would be for Rick to accept the idea he could be Josh's father. And maybe he wasn't. Maybe she was making life difficult for all sorts of people unnecessarily but she had no choice, did she?

This was about Josh.

Mike Randall was frowning. 'I'm confused,' he confessed. 'What's Rick got to do with this, Sarah?'

'Absolutely nothing.' Rick held up his hands in an eloquent gesture of denial. 'Look, I'm sorry,

Sarah. I've got no idea where this is coming from but you couldn't be more wrong.'

Sarah swallowed hard. She directed her next words at Mike rather than Rick. 'I was chasing someone I thought was called Richard. Known as Rick. I couldn't find any Richard. Then someone suggested that Rick could be short for Eric and…bingo.'

She heard an angry huff of sound from Rick. He turned, walked a couple of jerky steps, shoving his sleeves clear of his wrists as though preparing to do battle. Then he swung back to face them all, shaking his head incredulously.

'I mean, I know I haven't exactly been a monk but…for God's sake, I wasn't even in the country at the time Josh would have been conceived… what, eight or nine years ago? I was in Sydney on a postgraduate surgical course for two years. Wasn't I, Max?'

'Ah… Yes, but—'

'There isn't a "*but*".' Rick was staring at Max with lines of bewilderment creasing his face now. He was being attacked here. Where was the back-up he clearly expected? Max looked as though he was in physical pain. He wanted, more than anything, to be able to provide the support his friend desperately wanted but he couldn't do it because he knew something Rick didn't.

Sarah waited, knowing that Rick would turn back to her eventually. She was the one initiating this attack, wasn't she? So she watched him, seeing the way he straightened his spine and the way his hands curled into fists of frustration. It was the bewilderment that really got to her, though. A window of vulnerability in a man who might otherwise seem invincible. Big. Strong. Clever. Impossibly gorgeous right now with the sleeves of that dinner jacket shoved onto his forearms and the top button of his shirt undone with the ends of that black tie hanging on each side.

Sure enough, he turned to make eye contact with her and it was like a physical blow. As though she had betrayed him.

She had to swallow hard. 'How old do you think Josh is, Rick?'

'Seven,' he said promptly, dredging up another

fragment of a conversation in past weeks. 'Or maybe eight.' He flicked a challenging glance at Max.

'That's what I thought,' Max said apologetically. 'But it was a guess, Rick. I—'

'I know he's small for his age,' Sarah interrupted, trying to let Max off the hook. 'But he's nine. Coming up to nine and a half. He was conceived in Auckland a bit over ten years ago.'

Rick was still glaring at Max. 'You *knew* about this, didn't you?'

'Only since last night.' Max sighed heavily. 'It's not as if I've had a chance to talk to you. Sarah promised not to say anything until after the wedding. I was going to warn you, mate.'

Sarah caught Mike's glance. Friction on a personal level between these two men wasn't going to be helpful. He raised his eyebrows and Sarah nodded.

'I went to the States,' she said, 'to find the man who was on Josh's birth certificate. The man my sister genuinely thought *was* Josh's father as far as I could tell. He thought he might be, too and actually got excited by the idea. He couldn't wait to do the DNA test and he was gutted when it turned out that Josh couldn't possibly be his son.'

Rick snorted. 'You'll get the same result from me,' he said coldly. 'Except I won't be pretending *I'm* gutted.' He shook his head. 'You're wasting your time. And *mine*.'

Sarah was finding it hard to stay calm. He was simply going to refuse to accept the possibility, wasn't he? This might turn into a dead end that could haunt her for ever.

'My sister's name was Lucy,' she said with a tiny wobble in her voice. 'She was two years older than me and we looked very alike.'

He couldn't deny he found her attractive, surely? His interest had been flashing like a neon sign from the first moment he'd laid eyes on her. The kind of physical attributes people found attractive in the opposite sex didn't change that much. She had always been drawn to tall, dark men. Like Rick.

She sighed again, inwardly this time, at the regret that tugged deep inside. In another lifetime she might have been having a very different kind of conversation with Rick Wilson.

'Lucy Prescott?' she prompted. 'Ring any bells?'

'No.' The word was a growl.

'The man who wasn't Josh's father remembered her. It had only been a brief affair but he'd been in love with her. He'd said he'd known he was failing to measure up to the previous man in her life. Only a one-night stand, Lucy had said, and it was never going to go anywhere, but it was all too obvious that she would have preferred it to.'

And Sarah could understand why now. She could also begin to understand why her sister had always kept it a secret. A private fantasy that might have been discredited by sharing it with anyone, even her sister. Rick was one of a kind and he would have been completely out of her league back then when Lucy had been just a shy, country girl starting out on her nursing training.

'He went to the States a month or so later,' she finished. 'He never knew Lucy was pregnant. She refused to tell him. Or say who the father was. I only found that out when I requested Josh's birth certificate after he got sick.'

Silence fell as she finished speaking. Through the crack in the nearby door came a soft whimper.

Sarah tensed and then breathed out with a sigh of resignation. She had to go back to Josh, to be there when he woke up, but it wasn't as if there wasn't any point in saying anything more right now. She had dropped the bombshell. The best thing she could do was give Rick the space to get his head around it.

It was hard not to add a plea of some kind before she turned away. Especially seeing as Rick was giving her his undivided attention. Or maybe he was hoping he could make her go 'poof' and disappear from his life by sheer willpower. She held his gaze for a long second.

Please, she begged silently. *Just...please.*

Mike followed Sarah back into the room to check on his young patient and Rick was left in the corridor with just Max for company.

He turned on his heel and began to walk away.

'Hey...' Max sounded alarmed. 'Where are you going?'

'To find someone to talk to,' Rick snapped. 'A mate who might genuinely be in *my* corner.'

'*I'm* in your corner.' Max caught up with him well before he reached the elevators.

That hadn't been the impression he'd just got. Rick didn't pause to push the button or wait for a lift. He didn't want to give Max the chance to say anything else. Shoving the fire-escape door open, he took to the stairs, ignoring the sound of the footsteps following him. He didn't even look over his shoulder as he barged into the emergency department.

Jet was listening to a patient's chest in a cubicle near the internal doors. He glanced up, took in the expression on Rick's face and smoothly unhooked the earpieces to hang the stethoscope around his neck.

'You're quite right,' he said to the registrar beside him. 'Order a chest X-ray and start some diuretics. I'll be in the office for a few minutes.

Page me if I'm needed.' With a commanding jerk of his head, he led both Rick and Max into one of the consultants' offices.

'What the hell's the matter with you two?'

'Why don't you ask *him*?' Rick growled. He glared at Max.

Jet hooked one leg up to perch on the edge of the desk. He studied Rick for a moment and then turned his attention to Max. And then, surprisingly, he grinned.

'Takes me right back, this does. Remember when the headmaster caught you two fighting on the dorm floor? You got detention for a month and had to pick up rubbish on the rugby grounds. Matt and I used to fall over ourselves laughing, watching you with your spiky sticks and bags.'

His smile faded, his gaze settling on Max. 'What? What did I say?'

Max sighed. 'This has kind of got something to do with Matt, that's all.'

'For God's sake,' Rick exploded. 'How can you say that? It's got *nothing* to do with Matt.'

'Of course it has. And if you calmed down and

tried using your brain for half a minute, you'd see why. *Think* about it.'

'What does he need to think about?' Jet's tone was wary.

'Matt,' Max said heavily. 'What life was like for us all when he died.'

Rick looked up at the ceiling. He didn't realise how hard his fists were clenched until the ache reached his elbows.

Unbearable, that's what it had been like. Matt had been the final member of their group. The youngest by a few months and a bit smaller but he'd made up for his lack of height with an extra dose of daring and humour and intelligence. Life had been the ultimate adventure for Matt but he had died, tragically, when a brain aneurysm had not been diagnosed in time to save him, despite the warning symptoms. They had all been newly qualified doctors at the time. The remaining three, aching with such a loss, had all blamed themselves in some way for his death.

'You hit the books, I seem to remember,' Jet said slowly. 'We hardly saw you.'

'And you burned off your grief getting your black belt in that martial arts thing.' Max nodded. 'And Rick? Do you remember what he did?'

'Drank a lot,' Jet said promptly. 'And partied like there was no tomorrow.'

'Exactly.'

The satisfied note in Max's voice was more than irritating.

'There's no "*exactly*" about it,' Rick informed them. 'I'm careful. Even if I'm drunk I'm careful.'

'Can you honestly put your hand on your heart and swear there might not have been an occasion then when you found you didn't have anything on hand or were just too blasé to care?'

Rick said nothing. The truth was that that period of time was pretty much a blur now. He'd been trying to forget and it had been a successful mission. He closed his eyes slowly.

Too many parties. Too much alcohol. Way too many girls and most of them had been blue-eyed blondes. Max had married a woman with chestnut hair. Jet thought the darker the better but

Rick had always gone for blondes. That particular period wasn't an indication of how he usually
treated women, however, and even now he could
feel shame at the way he'd used those girls.

One-night stands had been all that he could
do. He'd had enough emotional rubbish to deal
with without inviting any more into his life. All
he'd wanted had been the temporary release that
sex could provide and if it wasn't enough for
the partner, she'd got brushed aside. Names? As
much of a blur as the faces. Pick a girl's name, he
thought wearily. Any name could be a contender.
Annabelle or Casey or Lisa or…or *Lucy*. Yes. If
Sarah's sister had been at one of those parties and
had been willing, he would have taken advantage
of her.

Of course he couldn't swear to anything and
his friends knew it. Maybe talking about this
wasn't such a good idea. It certainly wasn't helping. Any second now and Jet was going to be
taking the side Max was on. The dark side. Rick
needed to be alone. A stiff drink or two and
some peace and quiet and maybe he could parcel

up this feeling of dread and make it go away somehow.

'Condoms aren't a magic bullet, anyway,' Max continued. 'You know that. They can fail. Or break. How many times have we congratulated ourselves on our hassle-free record? Or so we thought.'

Jet whistled silently. 'Oh, man… Is this going where I think it's going?'

Max didn't seem to have heard him. He was still talking directly to Rick. 'Lucy looked just like her sister. Maybe your memory of ten-plus years ago is understandably hazy but what about a few hours ago? Your tongue was practically hanging out of your mouth the instant you clapped eyes on Sarah.'

'Sarah?' Jet was sitting very still now. Making sense of what was happening around him.

'Lucy was Sarah's sister,' Max said more quietly. 'Josh's mother.'

'Holy cow! And she thinks Rick's the father?'

'He could be,' Max agreed.

'She's wrong,' Rick said at the same time.

'How do you know?' Jet asked Rick.

'I just *do*.' Rick knew his tone was desperate. He didn't know, did he? He just couldn't begin to imagine the repercussions if she was right. To be presented with a nine-year-old kid? A *sick* kid? To know that the boy had been in the world for so long and he hadn't even known he'd existed? No. There was no way to get his head around this.

Max and Jet exchanged a glance.

'The solution's simple,' Jet said. 'Three letters, mate. DNA.'

Max stepped towards Rick and gripped his upper arm. 'He's right. The possibility is there and a kid's life might depend on it. If nothing else, you can set the record straight and Sarah can keep hunting.'

Yes. There was definitely a possibility there. One that might let him off the hook completely.

'Fine. I'll do the damn test.'

The thought that it might exonerate him kept him going until he reached home. The long hours of a solitary, sleepless night, however, put a far more negative spin on the plan.

Maybe fate had it in for him. Perhaps this was his punishment for that wild, irresponsible few months until he'd got both his head and his act back together. And what a punishment it would be. The effect it could have on his life was potentially catastrophic. Having a child could have a major impact on career choices, finances, relationships...

Being a father.

Oh, man...that was a minefield and a half. He couldn't do it. He had no idea of how a father should behave. He only had to think of his own father to know how they *shouldn't* behave but that was no help. His mates wouldn't be able to help either, would they? They'd all had way less than perfect family lives, which was why they'd all been sent off to boarding school and ended up forging their bond. The kind of family that meant something.

Max would think he'd know but he was getting in on the ground floor with Mattie, wasn't he? He hadn't been presented with a child who was old enough to judge performance and find it lacking. Old enough to get *hurt*, dammit.

It would be a disaster for everybody involved but most especially Josh, who most certainly didn't need that in his life on top of everything else. He couldn't do it to him. But if he did turn out to be Josh's father, he'd have no choice.

The endless merry-go-round of thoughts and emotions finally slowed as dawn broke and in those quiet minutes as a new day was born, Rick found a solution.

If his irresponsibility had created a child and fate had decreed that he could help him in some way, then of course he would do it. Josh didn't have to know where the bone marrow was coming from. If he didn't know that his biological father was involved, Rick wouldn't have to try and be the person Josh would want his father to be. He wouldn't have to hurt the kid by trying… and failing. It would be kinder all round, really.

Much kinder.

* * *

The attraction had been snuffed out. As cleanly as a lamp being switched off. There wasn't even a flicker of it to be seen when Rick came to the ward the following morning.

He didn't come into Josh's room. Just gave Sarah a curt nod through the window and then waited for her to join him in the relative privacy of the corridor.

'I've sorted the tests,' he told her. 'DNA, blood and tissue typing. You'll have to wait for the results.'

'Thank you.'

It was such an inadequate thing to say. She could see how huge this had been for him. Rick looked as though he hadn't slept a wink. There were shadows under his eyes and more lines around them than she remembered. It really wasn't fair that it only added to his appeal or that his appeal for her was still there when it had totally gone from his side of the equation.

She'd done her own share of thinking last night. Imagining Lucy with Rick. Feeling disturbingly…envious.

Just as well that Rick had shut off that static of sexual awareness. They could be colleagues now. A step up from total strangers but new enough to still have to earn trust. And that wasn't going to be easy because Rick's demeanour suggested she'd already had his trust and couldn't have broken it more effectively.

Fair enough. She had tipped his life upside down. Taken away his carefree existence. Put a huge spoke in the entire wheel of his universe, probably.

'Don't go getting your hopes up too much,' Rick warned.

'I won't. But…'

'But what?'

Amazing that his eyes could darken even further. They were like coals now. Remnants of a fire that had long since died out. Sarah had to look away.

'Have…have you given any thought to the next step, if…if…?'

Oh, Lord. She couldn't even say it out loud.

'If I do turn out to be his father?' Rick's mouth

curled but it couldn't be considered any kind of smile. 'Give me some credit, Sarah,' he drawled. 'I'm not stupid.'

'I wasn't suggesting you were.' The putdown sparked something that felt like rebellion. Didn't he know by now that she was more than prepared to fight for what was right?

'If I'm his father and there's enough of a match to make my bone marrow compatible, then of course I'll be a donor.'

Sarah let out a breath she hadn't noticed she'd been holding. This was precisely what she'd wanted to hear. So why was she left with this oddly unsatisfied sensation?

'If—and it's a mighty big *if* as far as I'm concerned,' Rick continued, his voice low and intense. 'If things do turn out that way and I'm a donor, then that's the end of it.'

'Sorry?' Sarah wasn't following.

'I had no idea he existed,' Rick said. 'He's nine years old. It's a bit late to step into the role of being a father. So I don't want Josh to be told. Is that clear?'

Sarah's mouth opened but no words came out.

It was clear all right. But acceptable? That was something else entirely. If she called him on this, however, he might back off and he'd already agreed to being a potential donor. That was all that mattered right now, wasn't it?

One step at a time.

It wasn't the first time in their brief acquaintance that she'd had the impression Rick Wilson was a man used to getting what he wanted from life.

He had taken her silence for acquiescence.

'Good,' he said. 'I'm glad we understand each other.'

And with that, he turned and left. Mission accomplished.

That spark of rebellion flared. Any kind of fan could easily see it flame into anger but Sarah had her own mission to deal with.

Intravenous sedation had made Josh sleepy enough not to notice his bed being wheeled into the treatment room of the ward. Or even being rolled onto his stomach and having the skin around his lower spine swabbed with disinfectant and then covered with a sterile drape that had a square hole in its centre.

Sarah positioned herself close to his head and took a small hand in hers.

'All set?' Mike was gowned and gloved. He had a syringe full of local anaesthetic in his hand.

Sarah nodded. She focused on Josh's face rather than watching the needle. She saw the crease on his forehead that let her know he was aware of his skin being pierced. The deeper frown and tiny whimper that told her the bone was now being frozen.

Despite the sedation and all the local anaesthetic, the next part of the procedure was painful. Not that Josh would remember any of it, thanks to the medication, but Sarah would. The sleepy groans and embryonic sobs brought tears to her own eyes and she ended up having to sniff audibly.

'You OK, Sarah?'

'Yes.'

'Not much longer.'

'That's good.'

It was probably just as well that Rick had backed away from any involvement with Josh at the moment. If he was watching this, he'd know exactly what was in store for him if it came to donating bone marrow. There'd be more than one puncture site, too, because they'd need a couple of litres of his liquid marrow. Josh only needed a tiny amount to cover the slides a technician was ready to prepare at the nearby trolley.

Would Rick opt for a general anaesthetic? Hardly likely, given the small but significant risk. IV sedation like Josh had had? That also didn't seem likely. He was a surgeon and having to abstain from making any important decisions or doing medical procedures might be a huge inconvenience. She wouldn't be at all surprised if he opted to just tough it out with local and that thought was enough to make her shudder inwardly.

She couldn't do it. Of course, it would be his choice but it was a lot to ask of anyone. Except that if it came to that, Rick wouldn't be just anyone. He'd be Josh's father. His *dad*. And it was a small thing to ask if it could save his son's life.

Mike had finished aspirating the marrow. Now he needed to do the biopsy.

'Almost done, short stuff,' Sarah whispered. 'You're being a wee hero.'

As he always was. He was such a brave kid. As if it hadn't been enough to lose his mum when he was only six and have to go and live with an aunt he hadn't seen nearly enough of. She wished she'd been there more for him when he'd been little but Lucy had gone back to their small home town after their mother had died and it had been her older sister who'd pushed her to stay in big cities and keep taking her career to the next level. Not to make the same mistakes she'd made.

At least she hadn't been a total stranger when tragedy had struck. Her love for Josh had been genuine but, even if she hadn't loved him as her nephew, he would have captured her heart totally over the last year with his courage and resilience.

'I'll get better,' he often reassured her. 'Don't

worry, Sarah. One day I'll be big and I'll look after *you*.'

Sarah had to sniff again. A nurse passed her a tissue and Mike looked up to give her a sympathetic smile.

'We're all done. Looks like a good sample. Not too much cortex.'

'Great.'

'We'll head on up for the MRI before the sedation wears off. I'll give him some pain relief, too. He'll be a bit sore when he wakes up.'

'He'll be OK,' Sarah said. 'I don't think he's ever really complained after one of these.'

Rick would be in even more pain after this procedure but he'd get over it soon enough and as far as he was concerned, that would be the end of his involvement. And…dammit, that really wasn't acceptable, Sarah realised.

'He's an amazing kid,' Mike was saying warmly as he pressed a gauze swab to the puncture site. 'One out of the box.'

So true. And if Rick was Josh's father, he needed to spend enough time with him to see what an incredible person his son was. Everyone who knew this child fell in love with him. Josh deserved to know that his own father was amongst that number.

If Rick thought he could make up for refusing to acknowledge his son merely by going through a medical procedure then he had another think coming his way, courtesy of her. *This* was what had been niggling at her ever since he'd walked off earlier. Where her anger was stemming from. He was dismissing Josh as a person without seeing how special he was. He should be *proud* to claim him.

And surely Josh had a right to know who his father was? But how could Sarah tell him if there was rejection in store?

One step at a time, she reminded herself, walking beside Josh's bed on their journey to the radiology department for the MRI scan. She squeezed his hand, reassuring herself as much as the drowsy child. The next step couldn't happen until the test results came through and that gave her plenty of time to think about exactly what that step should involve.

The thirteen-year-old boy lay, white and still on a bed in the intensive care unit. Flanked by monitors, IV tubing, medical staff and two distraught-looking parents.

The mother was crying again. The father put his arm around her. 'He's still alive,' he said, his voice raw. 'It'll be OK, you'll see. The doc knows what he's doing. It'll be OK.'

He looked down at his son but the glance was brief. The sight was still too horrific. The swathe of bandages around the head. Eyes so swollen you couldn't see eyelashes even, and then there was the awful bruising and a split lip to cap it off. He must be virtually unrecognisable even to his closest family.

This was the kind of case Rick found particularly gruelling. A whole family torn apart because of a dreadful accident. Simon had been on his way home from school and had been knocked off his bicycle by a speeding delivery van. He had a badly fractured leg, supported by a slab of plaster and padded by pillows until the boy's condition was stable enough for further surgery. It was much less of a concern than his head injury at this point in time. Right now, Simon was on a ventilator, unable to breathe on his own, and the surgery Rick had just performed held no guarantees for either survival or a good long-term outcome.

Simon's parents were a mess. Shocked and terrified but desperate to be with their son. This had to be every parent's worst nightmare and Rick had seen it all too often.

Was this why he'd never given serious thought to having a family of his own? He wasn't totally averse to the notion like Jet was, but neither could he imagine embracing the concept as Max had done. He was somewhere between the two. The desire was there but still dormant. Weighed down, perhaps, by the legacy of his own childhood.

Along with the logistics of attaining the state of parenthood, the motivation to deal with the downsides of parenting had made it all too easy to shove the whole concept into the 'too hard' basket and leave it there. And if it stayed in there so long it was too late to do anything about it, the whole issue might just quietly go away and he'd be able to take comfort in the thought that he couldn't have really wanted it badly enough in any case.

It was getting late by the time Rick left the ICU, but for a while he hung around the wards, reviewing his inpatients. He was reluctant to head home because it would mean a visit to his office to collect his keys.

Had it only been a few days ago when he'd been less than happy with the company of his mates and had wanted time alone to get his head sorted? Now, when he'd had enough of himself, there was no opportunity to obtain the kind of company he needed.

He'd assured Max that he would be absolutely fine. That Max couldn't possibly postpone the week in Rarotonga that he and Ellie and Mattie had lined up for their honeymoon. He'd meant every word of it at the time, of course, but then he hadn't known that Jet would receive a summons back to his elite army medical unit. A three-month stint that would see him involved in training exercises and deployment to any areas that might need the specialised skills of the unit. He'd left town yesterday, with his personal belongings in a backpack, his bike under cover in Rick's garage and the satisfied gleam of impending adventure lighting his features.

Rick had no one to talk to.

About the rough day he'd had at work.

Or about the envelope that had landed in his in-box this afternoon, seconds before the call to the emergency department where Simon had been waiting.

He knew what was in that envelope.

The DNA results.

The slip of paper inside could be a passport to freedom but it could also be a life sentence.

Being a father might not be a choice he had the luxury of making. It might be about to blindside him and, despite thinking he had found a solution that would work for everybody involved, he still had no idea how he was going to react if he discovered he really was Josh's father.

Maybe he didn't need his mates around to talk to. He could almost hear Jet's impatient voice.

Only one way to find out, man. For God's sake, just get on with it.

With a grim smile, Rick dropped the set of notes he was holding back into the trolley and headed for his office.

Minutes later, he was staring at his hands in disgust. He was a surgeon, for heaven's sake. With a reputation he could be justifiably proud of. He operated on people's brains and spines. Tricky surgery that required absolute precision and he'd never known his hands to falter. To tremble.

They were damn close to trembling now, as he ripped open that envelope.

CHAPTER THREE

'Do you want the good news or the bad news first?'

Josh rolled his eyes and sighed theatrically. 'Gimme the bad news, then.'

'You're in for new treatment stuff next week.'

'More chemo?'

'Yeah.' Sarah was trying hard to sound upbeat but it wasn't easy and she had to blink rapidly a few times. Josh was watching her.

'That's OK, I s'pose. Like last time?'

'Not exactly. They're going to bring the big guns out this time and try and shoot all the cancer cells. You'll get some radiation treatment as well as the drugs.'

Josh's eyes widened. 'I'm gonna be radiated? Will I go green or start glowing?'

Sarah grinned. 'No. And don't go expecting

to get some superpowers or anything, either. It's more like having a whole bunch of X-rays all at once.'

Josh was a smart kid. He understood far more than most people gave him credit for and Sarah had always been honest with him. Not that she gave him every detail, of course, but if he asked a question, she told him the truth. Josh seemed to know how much information he could handle and, like many children who faced life-threatening disease, he had a wisdom way beyond his years.

He put Sarah to shame, sometimes, with his acceptance of how things were. He understood death better than any child should. He wasn't afraid of it but he loved life and instinctively made the most of every moment. Right now, however, he was having a flash of being just an ordinary little boy and his bottom lip jutted out.

'Will it hurt?' he asked in a small voice.

'No.' Sarah badly wanted to gather him into her arms but she knew better. Josh was getting well past wanting hugs or slobbery kisses. She often caught hints of the man he could become, in fact. Like now, as he squared bony shoulders and lifted his chin.

'That's OK, then.' The glance he gave his aunt was steady. 'Is that it?'

'Not quite. You're going to have a Hickman catheter put in again.'

He'd had one before, in his first run of chemotherapy. The indwelling catheter would be inserted into a central venous line and stitched in place. It meant that all the drugs and blood products could be administered and samples taken without the pain or risk of infection that came from multiple puncture sites.

'But I'll be asleep when they do that, right?'

'Oh, yes. Of course.'

'Am I going to get real sick again?'

It was hard to maintain the direct eye contact. 'You might. They'll give you stuff to stop you throwing up.'

'Is this going to be the last time I have to do it?'

'We're all hoping so, hon.'

'When is it going to start?'

'Well, that's the good news. Not for a few days and you're allowed to come home until then. You get to choose whatever you want to do and we can go to the shops and get a supply of DVDs and books and anything else you want to bring into hospital with you.'

'They've got tons of stuff here already. Will I be in this room again or can I go in with the other chemo kids? Oscar's got ALL like me and he said there's an empty bed in his room.'

Sarah took a deep breath. The 'good' news had come and gone in a heartbeat. 'You won't be in this ward, Josh. You're going to a special unit. You'll have your own room and everything you need but it's...' Oh, God. How could she sound upbeat in telling him that he would be kept in strict isolation? For weeks? 'It's bug-free. To protect you from getting any kind of infection.'

'But I'm better. I haven't got a temperature or anything now.'

'This treatment is different. You know how

the bad leukaemia cells happen in your bone marrow?'

'Yeah. That's why they stick holes in my back. To get the marrow and look at the cells under the microscope and count them.'

'This new treatment is designed to get rid of all the bad cells but it kills off the good ones as well. Doctor Mike will be able to draw you some nice pictures of what happens but it means that, for a while, you won't have any bone marrow that does its job of making new blood or protecting you from bugs.'

'And then what happens?'

'They give you some new bone marrow. When it's had enough time to get right into your bones and settle down, it'll start making new blood. Nice, healthy blood.'

Josh took that in, frowning with concentration.

'So I'll be fixed?'

'That's the plan.' Sarah's smile broke through as she took out that shiny, new hope to show Josh. 'This is it,' she told him solemnly. 'The chance we've been waiting for.'

'So you've found my dad, then?'

Sarah's breath caught. She'd never told Josh that she was trying to trace his biological father. He'd never asked. As far as she'd known, he thought that the trip to the States had been so that he could go to Disneyland and the visits to a hospital and the doctor who used to live in New Zealand had been simply to look after him while they were away.

Had he overheard something?

Oh… Lord… Had he done more than play games on her laptop? Read her emails, maybe?

'Who is he?'

Still, words failed Sarah. Rick had made his wishes very clear on this subject. It wasn't that she didn't have the courage to defy him, more that she hadn't been able to come up with any plan that didn't involve Josh facing rejection, and she couldn't bring herself to inflict emotional pain on top of the physical ordeal he was facing.

'It's OK,' Josh told her kindly. 'I already know.'

'*What*?'

'It's Max's friend. The man at the wedding. Rick.'

Sarah's jaw dropped. 'How do you know that?'

'I heard you talking to Ellie. Promising that you wouldn't say anything until after the wedding. And…you kept looking at him kind of funny. Kept watching him.'

'Did I?' Sarah felt helpless. How on earth was she going to explain *this* to Rick? She could hardly expect him to believe that Josh had figured it out for himself without her saying anything. He'd be furious.

'How come he didn't know?' Josh asked.

'That he was your dad?'

Josh nodded.

'It happens.' This was more information than a nine-year-old should have to deal with. But Josh wasn't any-nine-year old, was he? 'A girl can get pregnant and have a baby but if she doesn't tell the father and they're not together any more, there's no way for him to know.'

'But he knows now?'

It was Sarah's turn to nod.

'Why hasn't he come to visit me, then?'

Good question. As good as the very similar one she'd asked Mike Randall herself, not very long ago, when the oncology consultant had been the one to tell her the amazing news of what a close genetic match Rick had turned out to be for Josh. But Mike hadn't been able to give her an answer and she had to be very careful with what she said to Josh.

'You know what?' she asked finally.

'What?'

'I think he's scared of you.'

Josh looked puzzled then shook his head. 'I'm just a kid. He's a grown-up and he rides a motorbike. Why would he be scared of *me*?'

'Being a parent *can* be scary,' Sarah tried to explain. 'Especially if it just happens. One minute you're not and then—*bang*—you've got someone else to be responsible for and take care of and… and love. It can change your whole life.'

'I s'pose.' Josh was watching her carefully. 'Were *you* scared of me?'

Sarah smiled. 'You bet I was. But I still wanted

you and you know I love you to little pieces, don't you?' She had to hug him now. And give him a big kiss on the top of his head.

Josh made a disgusted noise. 'He'll have to come and see me,' he said decisively when he had wriggled free.

'How's that?'

'When he gives me his bone marrow.'

Sarah was silent again. It was quite possible that the only part of Rick Josh would get to meet would be the bone marrow donated arriving for infusion. The frustration was familiar now, the anger still simmering quietly on Josh's behalf. The desire to protect this lad from rejection was redundant. The fact that he knew the identity of his father and was waiting for a visit that might never happen meant that the rejection was already real.

'You can tell him it's not so scary,' Josh said.

'Oh, Josh...' Sarah gave a huff of laughter. If only it was that easy. 'I will,' she promised, 'but don't get your hopes up too much. Rick might be more scared than I was and...it just happened for me, didn't it? You turned up on my doorstep, pretty much. And…' she smiled at this little boy with all the love in her heart '…it was the best present I ever, ever got.'

Josh's nod was thoughtful. 'Maybe you should give me to my dad, then,' he said calmly.

'*What*?' For the second time in the space of only minutes, Sarah was utterly shocked.

'Not for ever.' Josh was frowning again, thinking things through. 'If *he* found me on his doorstep, he might stop being scared.' Big, brown eyes were alight with sparks of both determination and what looked worryingly like hope. '*He* might think I was a good present, too.'

Sarah had to close her eyes. Out of the mouths of babes. The countless scenarios she had played with in the last few days paled in comparison to the bold genius Josh had just come up with. But she had to shake her head.

'He um…might not be too happy about that, hon.'

Except that she could hear Ellie's voice now. The conversation they'd had just before she'd taken off for her honeymoon. When she'd given her Rick's address in case she needed help while they were away.

He'll help if he possibly can, she had said with complete conviction. *He's a great guy. They all are. I'd trust any one of those three guys with my life. With Mattie's life.*

That's what Sarah would be trusting him with, wasn't it? Because Josh *was* her life these days.

'It'd be OK,' Josh was saying. 'He'd see I'm not so scary. And, besides, I'd kind of like a ride on his bike. He said I could have one.'

Sarah's eyes flew open. 'No way!'

Josh looked mutinous. 'You said I could do anything I wanted to do before I have to come back into hospital and I want to ride a bike.'

'Why? They're horrible, dangerous things.'

'Mum said my dad rode a bike. She said he had a leather jacket and he was the nicest, handsomest man in the world.'

Good grief... Had Lucy known the real identify of Josh's father all along? Or had she seen something in Josh as he'd grown older that had reminded her of the man who'd been her secret? Or…maybe…she'd just wanted to give him a hero image to feel proud of. Sarah could understand why. She could only hold her breath and hope like hell that Rick would live up to his status.

'I might die,' Josh said matter-of-factly. 'What if that happens and I never got to find out what it's like?'

Sarah groaned inwardly. Talk about emotional blackmail.

But Josh was grinning now. He had her over a barrel and they both knew it.

He'd been thinking about Simon when the doorbell rang.

His young patient in Intensive Care was starting to breathe on his own and it looked like he'd be able to come off the ventilator very soon. Survival was seeming more likely but at what cost? How brain damaged might he be? His parents had adapted to their new environment remarkably quickly and they'd actually been overjoyed at the news of progress today but how happy would they be further down the track if their son couldn't talk or walk? Or maybe not even recognise them?

To see the bright, inquisitive eyes of an intelligent child looking up at him when he opened the door was light years away from where his thoughts had been. It was so unexpected that Rick was totally floored. His brain was having difficulty joining the dots.

'Josh? What on earth are you doing here?'

'Sarah dropped me.'

'Huh?' Rick looked over the boy's head. A small, red car was at the end of his driveway. It was a tricky manoeuvre at this time of day to back out onto what was essentially a main road. It could well take a minute or two.

'I've come to visit,' Josh said.

Rick dropped his gaze. Josh had a look on his face that could only be deemed supremely confident. Triumphant, almost. It was a look that said, *You can't send me away cos I'm your son.*

He also had what looked suspiciously like an overnight bag at his feet.

'Hang tight for a tick, buddy.' Rick pulled his lips into the best semblance of a smile he could manage. 'I'll be right back.'

He'd never walked down that driveway with such powerful strides. Driven by outrage. What the *hell* did Sarah think she was playing at here?

He almost missed his opportunity. She didn't see him approaching because she was looking over her shoulder and she'd found a gap in the traffic and started to back out. As she turned the wheel to change direction, Rick stepped out in front of her car. It was a pretty stupid thing to do but Rick was past thinking clearly. Did he really think he could stop the vehicle from running him over by thumping his fist on the bonnet like that?

Whatever. It worked. Sarah jammed on the brakes and the car stalled with a lurch. Rick took another two strides that brought him to the driver's window, which had been rolled down to aid visibility. Sarah was staring straight ahead, still gripping the steering-wheel.

'What's going on here?' He kept his tone quiet. Deliberately dangerous.

Sarah flinched but didn't meet his unfriendly stare. 'Josh wanted to visit you.' Her voice was high and tight. 'He seems to think that you offered him a ride on your bike and he wants to take you up on it.'

This didn't make sense. When he'd suggested that at the wedding, Sarah had acted as if he was planning to murder her nephew. Not that he was going to be distracted by trying to find out why she'd changed her mind. There were more pressing issues to get sorted.

'So you just left him on my doorstep? What kind of guardian *are* you? What if you'd got the address wrong? If I hadn't been home?'

The flinch had become semi-permanent. Sarah radiated tension.

'I got Mike to check your roster. I already knew your address. And…and I waited until I saw you open the door.'

She slid him a sideways glance that was an oddly appealing mix of defiance and guilt. Rick recognised something in that glance from way back. Teenage stuff. When you were doing something you simply had to do but knew damn well you would get into trouble if you got caught. Again, Rick wasn't going to be distracted and certainly not by some misguided feeling of empathy for this woman.

'Is this some kind of game? You think I'm going to change my mind about telling him I'm his father just because we're face-to-face?'

Sarah turned her head this time. He could see the movement of muscles in her throat as she swallowed. 'You don't have to change your mind. Josh already knows.'

Rick made an incredulous sound. 'You *told* him? After I specifically said that I didn't want—'

'No,' Sarah interrupted fiercely. 'I didn't tell him. I thought he had a right to know but I didn't tell him because I didn't want him to know that you didn't want to acknowledge him. Josh told *me* and I couldn't lie about it.'

Something cold was folding itself around Rick.

Fear? Or maybe it was actually something hot. Like fury.

'I don't believe you.'

'Your prerogative.' Sarah's tone was clipped. 'But for what it's worth, Josh wanted to meet you. This was his idea.'

'It's a very *bad* idea.' Rick's words were just as clipped as hers had been. 'I don't like being pushed around.'

'No. I don't suppose you do.'

Another glance and he had the impression there was a spark of…what, sympathy in her eyes? It *could* be amusement. Rick's anger strained at the leash.

'Did it not occur to you the risk you were taking? I'm not exactly happy about this, Sarah. What if I back out of this whole donor thing?'

'You wouldn't do that.'

Her calm assumption only pushed him further.

'How can you be so sure of that?'

His menacing tone did the trick. He saw the flash of fear in her face. Oddly, getting the upper hand wasn't as satisfying as it could have been.

'I'm trusting my instinct,' Sarah admitted. 'I don't think you're someone who'd break a promise.'

She wasn't talking about an offer to give a kid a ride around the block on the back of a bike here and they both knew it. Of course he wouldn't back out of being a donor when a life was at stake but this had just become a lot more complicated.

Messy.

Full of emotional fishhooks that Rick could already feel catching in his gut. And he was angry. Angry at having his life disrupted by having to think about any of this at all. At being manipulated by a woman and a kid who were making assumptions when they didn't know him at all. He didn't want them to know him, he realised. That was what this was all about. If he let them into his life, nothing would ever be the same.

He was fighting for his life here. Life as he knew it, anyway. And he had the horrible feeling that he wasn't going to win this battle. He folded his arms and stared down at Sarah. The anger was still fierce.

'Bit of a gamble, though, isn't it?'

'Yeah…' Sarah's tone hardened, as though she was catching his anger. Or maybe because she was disappointed in what he was revealing about his character. 'I'm gambling on you being a decent human being.'

He'd used those words himself to assure her that Josh's father, if he was located, wouldn't be able to refuse to do the right thing. Sarah's tone suggested that she was prepared to find out she'd been mistaken in believing him. That he was about to break her trust.

The car was making a partial obstacle on the road. A motorist made a point of coming to a halt and leaning on his horn to advertise the inconvenience. Rick was still stinging from Sarah's tone. He turned to glare at the driver and the man shook his head and pulled out to go around them.

'If you back out,' Sarah told him, 'Josh will die. I'll be working at Queen Mary's and you'll be reminded of him—and what you didn't do—every time you see me.'

'I could go somewhere else.' Rick knew he sounded immature. Petulant almost but there was something close to desperation hovering over him. There was a small boy on his doorstep right now who knew that Rick was his biological father. When he went back up that driveway, he would *be* a father, whether he wanted to be or not.

Sarah's gaze had softened. There was definitely sympathy in her eyes. 'You'll still remember,' she said quietly. 'Probably every time you see a kid.'

Another car went around them. Sarah was fiddling with her gear stick. Putting the car in neutral. Preparing to start it again and drive away?

'What on earth do you think you'll achieve by leaving him *here*? Just how long were you planning to abandon him?'

Sarah answered his second query first. 'Josh was going to text me. I would have come back very soon if he wasn't happy. What did I think I might achieve?'

Sarah's gaze was locked on his and Rick couldn't break the contact. 'Josh has the right to know what kind of person his father is. *You* need to know what you're missing out on if you don't know what kind of person your son is.' She gave a heavy sigh. 'You're already involved in this, Rick. I think you need to be invested in it as well.'

'Why? He's got you. That's been enough so far. It's still enough.'

'No. It isn't.' Sarah's voice rose. 'Not for Josh *or* for me.' Her voice shook now and her eyes flashed. 'Have you any idea how much I've been ripped apart by all this? No, of course you don't. You'd rather not even think about it. Keep it all at a nice, safe distance. Well, let me tell you something...'

She sucked in a quick, shaky breath. 'This sucks. You said you don't like being pushed into things. Newsflash, Rick—none of us do. And what did I get pushed into? Not only being a parent but having to deal with the kind of things that no one wants to face. It's not that I don't love Josh. He's a loveable kid and I adore him but it *hurts* like hell watching him go through all this. Knowing he might die in the end in spite of it.'

Sarah had tears on her face. She scrubbed at them angrily. 'I'm only his aunty,' she said, her voice raw. 'You're his *father*.'

Still, there was no way Rick could break that eye contact. Spare himself the accusation in her face.

'Grow up and take some responsibility,' Sarah snapped, turning the key and revving the engine of her car. 'You owe this much to Josh. Hey… maybe you owe it to me, too, for doing *your* job for so long.'

It was Sarah who broke the eye contact. The car was moving now and all Rick could think to do was to step back and let it go.

And when it had gone, he had a clear view up his driveway.

To where a small boy was sitting on his doorstep.

* * *

Sarah had to pull off the road just as soon as she could find a space that would be out of sight.

She could barely see with the tears flooding her eyes and her hands were shaking so hard she couldn't steer the car safely.

Having come to a halt, she sat there, gripping the wheel with both hands together at the top, her forehead resting on them.

What she'd just done—leaving Josh alone with Rick—was the hardest thing ever and she wasn't even sure she should have done it.

The thought of Josh being given a ride on Rick's motorbike was bad enough. Terrifying. His body was so fragile and would be far too easy to break. But leaving him with a man who could break his heart was infinitely worse.

She couldn't even stay and watch because if she had, the whole point of this exercise would have been negated. So she couldn't know what was happening and all she could do was wait.

She had to have faith, she told herself.

And she did. She had the utmost faith in Josh. In his intelligence and courage and maturity.

As her sobs subsided and she got her breathing under control again, Sarah was aware of something else.

For some unknown reason, she also had faith in Rick.

CHAPTER FOUR

THE confidence had vanished from Josh's face.

He couldn't have overheard anything that had been said down at the end of the driveway and he couldn't have even seen any facial expressions because Rick had been bending down on the far side of the vehicle and Sarah had turned in his direction, but he must have sensed the tension and he would have seen the car driving away. Had he noticed that Sarah hadn't given him a backward glance?

It might explain why he was looking so bereft.

Rick felt an odd pang in his chest that morphed into a kind of squeeze. He took in how pale Josh was. How he had less hair than he'd had even a few days ago. This kid was sick. There was a real possibility that he could die in the not-too-distant future and he was, essentially, an orphan.

You'd have to have a pretty black heart not to respond to that package. And he might look a bit lost and vulnerable right now but he still looked determined.

Rick felt his lips twist into a lopsided grin. He had to admire the kid's guts. Not to mention his enterprise. If he could apply the same tactics to beating his disease as he must have to get something he wanted—like the bike ride—he might have a good show of succeeding.

The car had taken Sarah away physically. Rick was making a supreme effort, as he walked back up the driveway, to push her out of the considerable mental space she was still occupying. This was about him and Josh. It would be totally unacceptable to take out any of his anger for Sarah on this child.

This was no big deal, really. It wouldn't even take that long. He'd give him what he wanted and then Josh could text his aunt and get taken home.

'A bike ride, then?' he offered.

OK, maybe he was sidestepping the major issue

here but he could hardly jump right in and talk about their biological relationship. Josh wasn't to know that *he* knew Josh knew the truth and at least he could sound casual about a bike ride. Friendly, even.

'Yeah…' That lost look was wiped from Josh's face as he grinned. 'That'd be awesome.'

'You'd better come inside, then, and dump your bag.'

The loft apartment was a warehouse conversion and the door led into a massive living area with a wall of glass that looked straight down on a busy wharf. Container ships were being loaded and unloaded. Trucks and cranes and forklifts and people wearing hard hats and bright orange high-visibility vests made the scene a hive of activity. Josh walked over to the windows and his jaw dropped. Rick was happy to let him stand there and take it in.

He needed a moment himself. He walked to the kitchen that was part of the open-plan area and eyed the bottle of beer he'd uncapped just before the doorbell had sounded. With a sigh of regret he screwed the cap back on and put it back in the fridge. It would have to wait until after the joy ride and by then he might need something a good deal stronger. He took a sideways glance at the small boy, who was still staring at the view with rapt attention.

A small boy's dream, having something like this to watch on tap. Was that why he loved it? Had he never really grown up? Sarah's stinging words were still sounding in his head.

Grow up and take some responsibility.

Maybe she had a point.

With an inward sigh this time, Rick pushed himself to walk closer to Josh. It felt incredibly awkward, which was weird because he was good with kids, but this was different. Hugely different. Unprecedented. It became slightly easier when he wasn't looking directly at Josh. They stood side by side to admire the view.

'Pretty cool, huh?'

'What's that little boat doing?'

'That one's a tug. It'll be going out to the heads to guide another big ship in. The one over there is the coastguard boat. They go out for rescues sometimes in really rough weather. That's fun to watch.'

Josh nodded but was busy watching massive logs being taken off the back of a truck. A crane was attached to chains in the middle of the logs and they tipped like a seesaw. 'What happens if they drop them?'

'It could cause a nasty accident, I guess. But they know what they're doing. I've never seen them drop any yet.'

Josh looked as though he could happily stand there for a long time but Rick was feeling edgy. Too aware of this small person standing so close. Of the fact that they were alone together. That he might have to talk about the fact that he was Josh's father.

'How 'bout that ride, then?'

'OK. But I don't mind waiting. If you're busy or something.'

'Nah. We can't go too far, though. It'll be getting dark before too long and I don't want you getting too cold or anything.'

'Where's your bike?'

'There's a garage space underneath here. The stairs are over by the kitchen bit.'

'Do you live here by yourself?'

'At the moment, I do.' Rick led the way to the internal stairwell. 'Max used to live with me and so did Jet.'

'Who's Jet?'

'You sat beside him at Max and Ellie's wedding. He was holding the baby.' The memory cheered Rick up but it also reminded him of the moment he'd set eyes on Sarah. Still being mad at her didn't seem to diminish his appreciation of the way she looked. She was gorgeous. Her sister had probably been gorgeous as well but to his shame Rick had no concrete memory of her. As he'd had to concede she would have been one of many in that period of his life he had no desire to remember in too much detail.

'Where is he now?'

'He had to go back to the army. He works as a doctor for the soldiers sometimes. Rides around in helicopters and rescues people and stuff.'

'Wow. That'd be cool.'

'Bikes are cool, too. See?' Rick stepped into the garage. This was another big space. His SUV for routine travel was parked on one side and on the other his bike stood in solitary, gleaming black glory. 'It's a Ducati,' he told Josh. 'Sportclassic GT1000. Not bad, huh?' He stroked the seat. 'Jet's got a Superbike, which is over there under the tarp while he's away. It's a bit more powerful but this is my baby.' He pulled his hand away from the machine with a final pat and then looked up to find Josh looking at him rather intently. Curiously.

As though he was behaving in an unexpected way. Was it possible Sarah had told him that she thought Rick had a lot of growing up to do?

'We'll need to give you a jacket and helmet,' he went on hurriedly. 'We'll use Jet's, he won't mind. They'll be miles too big for you but we can pad up the helmet and that's the most important bit of protection.'

Josh looked like a little kid playing dress-up by the time Rick had him kitted out to his satisfaction. His hands were lost in leather mittens and barely emerged from the sleeves of the jacket. His head was equally lost in the helmet and all Rick could really see was a pair of dark eyes staring at him as he rolled the bike out of the garage.

'Sarah says that motorbikes are horrible, dangerous things,' he informed Rick.

'Sarah's not a boy,' Rick responded, as though that excused her.

She wasn't a girl, either, he thought as he helped Josh climb onto the back of the bike. She was all woman, was Sarah. He was still puzzled as to why she was allowing this ride to go ahead. She'd be terrified that Josh would get hurt. The fact that she could put her own fears to one side to let Josh do something he wanted to do said a lot about her strength of character.

That she was letting him be the one to give Josh the ride said a lot about how much she was trusting him. Rick wasn't about to let her down.

'Put both arms around my waist and hang on

tight,' he instructed Josh. 'Don't let go for any reason, OK?'

'OK.'

'We're not going very far. We'll get a bit closer to the wharf so you can see the ships and then we'll go up the hill but that's all. And we're not racing anything. Got it?'

'Yep.' Josh's skinny arms came around Rick's waist and the grip was reassuringly strong. 'Let's go.'

They went.

Sarah wasn't any closer to getting home.

She was still sitting in her car in the lay-by but she wasn't crying any more. Staring out at the choppy, grey water of the harbour was soothing. Knowing that she was still close enough to Rick's apartment to go and rescue Josh in a matter of minutes was even more comforting.

Besides, she had a lot to think about. She could make a mental list of everything she needed to get done in the next couple of days. Washing and ironing so that Josh could pack everything he would need to move into the bone-marrow unit. Sorting the games and books and DVDs he'd want for the next few weeks. Shopping for treats. Arranging schoolwork, perhaps. And then there were all the other things that were a level away from Josh but still vital. Stuff that needed doing around the apartment. Going to the bank to try and arrange another loan. Paying the bills that were mounting up by the day.

She had to go back to work soon. A lot sooner than she might have chosen to but they weren't going to survive financially if she didn't. The trip to the States and then staying in Auckland had virtually wiped out her savings. If Josh settled well enough in the unit she might be able to start doing some shifts at night while he was asleep. It could be the ideal time in some ways, because he would have expert care when she wasn't around.

That wouldn't be on tap when he came out. Even if the bone marrow took successfully, he wouldn't be able to attend school normally for months yet. Paying someone to be with him while Sarah worked might take so much out of what she'd be earning that it would be pointless.

One day at a time.

The mantra arrived automatically these days, when the spiral of thoughts and worries threatened to overwhelm her. All that mattered right now was tackling this next, huge hurdle. When they were through it would be the time to worry about what was going to happen next. Sarah was practised in reversing the time telescope. She shrank it from the months ahead to weeks. Then into days and finally only hours.

Josh was with Rick. He was probably on the back of some horribly big motorbike while she was sitting here watching seagulls bobbing on tiny waves. She hoped he was hanging on tight. *She* certainly would be.

In fact, she could imagine it. Pressing against the solid back of Rick's body, her arms around his waist and the hum of a powerful engine beneath them. Bizarrely, the notion wasn't nearly as alarming as it should be. Instead, it had an appeal strong enough to quicken her pulse and send a curious warmth into her limbs.

A huff of laughter escaped Sarah. If she went any further down that track, it would be her begging for a ride next. But at least the awful tension was easing and she felt better. Not relaxed enough to want to drive the fifteen kilometres or so to her apartment in the city but more than enough to start wondering if she'd been a bit too hard on Rick.

Had she really told him he needed to grow up?

That he owed her something because she'd been doing his job as the sole parent figure for Josh?

That was unfair, given that he hadn't known of his child's existence.

He was a bachelor. One with a demanding job and probably precious little free time to enjoy other things like his bike. Or his home. Sarah hadn't taken much notice of her surroundings in finding Rick's address but now she found herself curious. Why did he choose to live out here? In what looked, from the outside, like an old warehouse? The whole area had given an impression of being old. Kind of rundown, which didn't quite gel with the image she had of Rick being a glitzy, playboy type.

It wouldn't hurt to go back, would it? To drive around and see if she'd missed something? She might find a café somewhere that could provide a good cup of coffee and, heaven knew, she could do with a caffeine boost. It would distract her for a while, too. If she hadn't received a 'come and get me' text from Josh within the next hour or so, she could assume that the visit was going well and then she would drive home and throw herself into some housework or something.

Sarah checked the road in both directions, put on her indicator and did a U-turn.

For the first time ever, Rick was feeling nervous about riding his beloved bike.

Good grief…even when he'd had his first solo ride when he'd been fifteen he hadn't felt like this. So aware of the unforgiving tarmac laid out beneath the speeding wheels. Padded leather could only do so much to protect skin and flesh and wasn't much protection at all when it came to broken bones. And how many head injuries had he dealt with over the years resulting from accidents involving motorbikes?

If Jet could see him riding this cautiously, he'd be grinning from ear to ear. Making some smart remark about him trading in the Ducati for a walking frame. But Jet had never taken a kid as a pillion, had he?

It felt weird. Nothing like any of the girls Rick had taken for a ride. Weightwise, he could have been alone so it made no difference to cornering or anything. He was acutely aware of the arms around his waist. A sensation that had always been a bonus with a pretty girl on the back, but this was a kid.

His kid.

Those tiny arms felt like prison walls. Starting to close in and trap something that was unrecognisable but important and Rick had the sinking feeling that it could be a big ask to ensure its freedom. The sooner this was over with the better.

They went as close to the wharf as they could get and went past acres of stored containers. He took them along the coast road for a mile or two after that, heading for Carey's Bay. Traffic was light and the road conditions were good and Rick found himself relaxing a bit. If they had more time, he thought, they could have gone a lot further. There were some fabulous beaches out this way, like Long Beach and Warrington and Murdering Beach. Surf and huge sand dunes that you could bodysurf down.

What was he thinking? Josh was nowhere near well enough to go swimming or play in sand dunes and he didn't want to spend hours in his company anyway. He turned them around and headed up a hill to give them a good view of the harbour and the bush-clad hills and crowded streets of Port Chalmers and then headed back.

The seaport was really a suburb of the city of Dunedin but it was more like a quirky little township in its own right. Industrial, thanks to the busy port, but it was also trendy for those wanting a slightly alternative lifestyle. It attracted artists and musicians. Very close to all the city amenities but most definitely outside its limits. On the edge, and Rick loved it.

He took them along Beach Street and then George Street, through the small town centre with all its cafés and galleries. He felt Josh loosen his grip around his waist. Fortunately, he was coming to an intersection when he needed to stop and give way. Before he could turn and tell Josh to hang on tightly again, he felt a small fist thumping his back.

'What's up, buddy?'

'That's *Sarah's* car,' Josh shouted.

'What? Where?'

Josh pointed. Then he waved.

With a sinking heart, Rick looked from the small car to the window of the café it was parked in front of. Sure enough, sitting on a high stool in front of a counter in the window was Sarah. Staring back. Looking as though she'd been caught out. Completely busted, no less.

The reddened cheeks and guilty expression made a nice change. Put Rick back on the moral high ground, even. He revved the bike engine gently. Just enough to give him the momentum to turn and roll into the vacant spot beside Sarah's car. It was too tempting not to rub her nose in it just a little.

'Let's go and say hello,' he suggested to Josh. 'I could do with a coffee.'

Sarah had known it was them as soon as she'd seen the bike rolling past the café window, slowing down for the intersection. Her heart had skipped a beat, seeing the reality of the small figure on the back of the black monster of a bike.

Josh had spotted her and there had been that awful moment of waiting for Rick's head to turn, knowing that he would think she was hanging around, spying on his lifestyle if not his person.

Her discomfort increased when she saw him turn the bike and park beside her car. Then he got off and pulled off his helmet and she saw this rugged man in his leather jacket and pants and heavy boots. The dark hair all tousled from the helmet removal. She couldn't drag her gaze away as he stripped off his gloves and stuffed them into the helmet. He wasn't smiling as he reached to lift Josh from the back of the bike but, perversely, that only made him seem more attractive.

A bad-boy biker. Dark and dangerous. But she could see the care he took in lifting Josh. The way he made it seem no big deal and not a putdown because of the boy's size or physical capabilities. Sarah's breath caught in her throat somewhere. She hardly knew Rick but she was getting the distinct impression that he was something rather unique. Special.

Josh looked tiny in his oversized clothes, needing both arms to carry the helmet inside, but there was something about them being dressed alike. It was more than the clothes, as it had been at the wedding. Something about the way they walked, maybe. An air of owning the space they were moving through. Sarah had the strange feeling that she was merely a guest in *their* café.

That she was privileged to be here, in fact. Even the smiles that the man and boy greeted her were oddly similar.

I did it, Rick's said. *See? I'm not as bad as you think I am.*

I did it,' Josh's said. *See? It's not as dangerous as you thought.*

Rick ordered a short, black espresso and didn't add any sugar. The remains of Sarah's sweetened cappuccino suddenly seemed frivolous and feminine. Josh opted for a milkshake but Sarah shook her head when he asked if he could have some food from the cabinet.

'It's not that long till dinnertime,' she said, despite feeling like a party-pooper. 'You need proper food, not cakes.'

'What's on the menu, then?' Rick queried.

They had taken the other stools at the counter and sat in a row, with Josh in the middle, but the boy was leaning forward, intent on holding his straw with no hands so Sarah and Rick had an almost clear space between them. Close enough to touch each other if they reached out, Sarah surprised herself by noticing.

'Whatever Josh fancies,' she said hurriedly. 'As long as it's real food and not junk.'

'A hamburger,' Josh said. 'They never give you hamburgers in hospital.'

'Hmm.' Sarah put off having to debate the nutritional value of Josh's choice. She smiled at him instead. 'How was the ride, short stuff?'

'Awesome. We went *really* fast.'

She couldn't help firing an accusing glare at Rick but he was shaking his head slowly, unseen by Josh. The wry smile made it perfectly convincing.

'I like the jacket.'

'It's Jet's. He's away rescuing soldiers in a helicopter.'

'Wow. That sounds exciting.'

'You should see Rick's house, Sarah. He gets to watch the ships and cranes and everything. It's cool.'

'Is it?' Sarah avoided looking at Rick this time. He might think she was angling for an invitation to visit his home. And she wasn't. This was about him and Josh. She was only involved as a facilitator and that was fine by her.

Absolutely fine.

Had he said anything to Josh about their relationship? Unexpectedly, Rick saw the question in her gaze, as though he could read her thoughts. He looked uncomfortable and the subtle movement of his head was negative. Sarah jerked her gaze away, disappointed.

A silence fell. Josh's initial enjoyment of the milkshake had waned and he seemed to become aware of the silence around him.

'I have to go back into hospital on Monday,' he announced.

'I know,' Rick said.

Of course he did. He would have an appointment to have his bone marrow collected within days of Josh's admission. He was watching Josh at the moment, his expression curious.

'Do you know what's going to happen this time?'

'Yeah. I'm gonna get radiated. I'll prob'ly go green and start glowing.'

Rick grinned. 'Maybe you'll get a superpower at the same time and be able to hear stuff from miles away.'

'Or go invisible.' Josh nodded. 'Or fly. That'd be cool.'

'Sure would. Closest I get to flying is going fast on my bike.'

'Like *we* did.'

'Mmm.' Rick's glance at Sarah assured her he was only agreeing so he didn't shoot Josh down. 'Do you know why you're getting the radiation?'

'To kill my bone marrow,' Josh told him. 'I've got ALL. D'you know what that is?'

'Tell me,' Rick invited.

There was genuine interest in his tone. He wanted to know how much Josh knew about his illness. Sarah peered into her coffee cup and caught a bit of leftover cinnamon dusted froth on her finger. She licked it off and went back for more.

'It's acute lymphoblastic leukaemia,' Josh said

with careful pronunciation and obvious pride in his ability to remember.

'What's that?'

Josh rolled his eyes. 'You should know. You're a doctor.'

Rick grinned. 'I do know. I was just wondering if *you* knew.'

''Course I do. I've got it.' Josh sighed with exasperation but co-operated anyway. 'It means that my white blood cells are wonky and I get too many of them, which means there's no room for good blood cells and it makes me really sick.'

Rick nodded. 'Wish they'd made it sound that easy at med school.'

'I might get fixed this time,' Josh continued. 'Because if I get good bone marrow, it might make white cells that aren't wonky.'

Sarah watched Rick drain his small coffee cup as though he needed fuel.

'It's my bone marrow that you'll be getting,' he said to Josh. 'It's always done a pretty good job for me.' A muscle in his jaw bunched. 'You know why it's *my* bone marrow that you'll be getting, Josh?'

'Yeah. You're my dad.'

The statement was completely matter-of-fact but it hung in the air with all the presence of an unexploded bomb. This could be it, Sarah realised, unable to expel the breath she'd sucked in. Josh could be in for a rejection of anything but a genetic similarity.

'Yeah…' Rick said quietly. 'I'm your father.'

The correction was subtle but significant. A dad was involved. Part of the son's life. A father didn't have to be.

'I never knew,' Rick added.

'I know.'

'It's been a bit of a surprise, really.'

'I know that, too.' Josh tilted his head to scrutinise Rick's face. 'I don't think you're really scared, though.'

'Who said I was?'

Josh turned away, clearly avoiding the need to make a response. He stared out of the window and his face suddenly lit up.

'Look at that dog, Sarah.'

She looked. The dog was large and very scruffy. It sat on the footpath with its nose almost touching the glass, staring up at Josh.

'Isn't it *cool*?'

'Hmm.'

'Can I go and pat it? *Please*?'

'Josh, you know you have to be careful of—' *Bugs*, she stopped herself saying. *Infection that could kill you so fast you wouldn't know what hit you.* 'Strange dogs,' she carried on in a slightly strangled voice. 'They might bite.'

'*He* wouldn't bite,' Josh said with absolute conviction. 'Look at him.'

She took a second glance. The dog's tongue was hanging out. Its tail was sweeping a patch of the footpath clean. Josh was sliding down from his stool and Sarah was aware of Rick's stillness. She could feel him staring at her. Clearly, he hadn't been distracted by the dog's appearance and was still stewing about who had told Josh he was a coward. Maybe an apology of some sort was due.

'OK,' she told Josh. 'Just for a minute, though, and be *careful.*'

The small boy streaked out of the door. Sarah met Rick's gaze.

'I told Josh how scary it was to have a kid land on your doorstep,' she said cautiously. 'To have your life tipped upside down and everything.'

Rick's closed expression was a warning that he had no intention of letting that happen. It was a clear reminder of the terms he had set out and let her know that if the repercussions of those terms being broken were unfortunate, it wasn't going to be his fault.

Sarah merely raised an eyebrow to remind him that the repercussions would affect him as well.

They both looked out of the window to where Josh was crouched beside the dog, hugging it. The dog wriggled with joy and sent a vast, pink tongue across the boy's face. Sarah couldn't help herself. She leaned forward and knocked on the window, shaking her head as Josh looked up. She could see the huge sigh he heaved and the difficulty with which he prised himself away from the dog. He even went back for a final stroke before he came back into the café. The dog watched until the door swung shut and then trotted away out of sight.

'Come and finish your milkshake,' Sarah told Josh. 'We should probably head home. We've got a big day tomorrow.'

'He didn't have a collar,' Josh said unhappily. 'And he shouldn't be running around on the road by himself, should he?'

'Lots of dogs do that around here,' Rick said. 'I wouldn't worry about it, buddy.' He raised an eyebrow at Sarah, which seemed like a query about whether it would be a good idea to change the subject. Her nod of agreement was subtle.

'So what's on the agenda for tomorrow?' Rick asked brightly.

'Shopping, mainly,' Sarah responded. 'We've got some Harry Potter episodes to stock up on amongst other supplies. And I'm going to try and get hold of Josh's teacher, Miss Allen, to get some work to pass on to the hospital tutor.'

'What?' Josh stopped leaning on the counter

to peer hopefully out the window. He sounded aggrieved. 'Do I have to do extra schoolwork?'

'You don't want to get too far behind, do you? For when you go back to school?'

'I s'pose not. The other kids would think I'm dumb.'

'You're not dumb, buddy.' Rick's statement was firm and Sarah could see the way Josh straightened his back with pride.

'Can we get a hamburger on the way home?'

'Maybe.'

'You said I could have whatever I wanted.'

'As long as it's proper food. Hamburgers are more like junk.'

'Not all of them,' Rick put in. 'There's a gourmet hamburger joint not too far from where we're sitting, in fact.'

Sarah frowned. Was he trying to undermine parental boundaries that were hard enough to get established anyway?

'You get things like fresh chicken breast with avocado and bacon,' Rick said calmly. 'Or steak. The one I like is grilled lamb with mint and cucumber yoghurt. And you can get kumera wedges instead of chips.'

Sarah's mouth was watering.

'I just want an ordinary hamburger,' Josh complained.

'These are better,' Rick said in a tone that brooked no further argument. 'Healthier. You can still get a beef and cheese burger.'

'You seem to know the menu off by heart,' Sarah said.

Rick shrugged. 'Jet and I didn't always have the time or inclination to cook. And these are seriously good, take my word for it.'

But Sarah looked at her watch. 'I don't think we can,' she said. 'We need to get your bag, Josh. You're due for all your pills.'

Rick barely hesitated. 'How 'bout we all grab some burgers and take them back to my place?'

Sarah's hesitation was far more pronounced but Josh was nodding vigorously.

'Yeah…that's what *I* want to do. Please, Sarah? Can we? We might see that dog again near the hamburger shop.'

* * *

It had been the polite thing to do, inviting them back.

Maybe the invitation had been a form of expressing his relief at how easily a potentially awkward situation had come and gone.

Josh simply accepted the fact that Rick was his father as steadily as he appeared to deal with his illness. No recriminations. No promises extracted regarding future involvement.

It was easier to get along with the boy than his aunt but what prompted the invitation also included a kind of peace treaty. He could let go of the anger he'd been holding for Sarah. Yes, she had pushed him. Manipulated him. But he'd never have offered to spend time with Josh voluntarily, would he? And now it was done and there were no dark secrets and it all seemed much more straightforward and less threatening.

She had done the right thing, with no assistance from him, and Rick could only respect that.

So, here they all were, lounging in the comfortable armchairs near the window, eating the enormous burgers and watching the lights come on all over the wharf as work continued into the night.

A bit different from sitting here with his mates, as he'd done so many times in the past, but it wasn't as bad as he'd thought it could be. The company was quite pleasant, in fact. Not that he'd want it all the time, of course, but…now and again didn't seem like it would be too much of a hardship.

Especially if Sarah came with Josh. There was most definitely a pleasure to be found in watching her. Rick knew he was going to be haunted later by the memory of her sitting in that café, sucking coffee froth off her finger. There was a slight moral dilemma here, in that he knew it wasn't exactly appropriate to find himself turned on by his newfound son's guardian, but he'd grapple with that later as well. As long as he didn't act on it, and kept hold of the new level of respect he had for Sarah, it was probably no problem.

They left soon after eating because Josh was clearly exhausted. Rick followed them out. Sarah got Josh installed in the front passenger seat and his eyes were closing even as she shut the door. Rick touched her shoulder to make her pause before she headed for the driver's seat.

'Is he OK?'

'He'll be tired out. It's been quite a day for him.'

Rick could understand that. It had been quite a day for him as well. 'This stuff you're going shopping for tomorrow?'

'Yes?'

'They're things Josh will need for his stay in hospital?'

'Yes.' Sarah was watching him, her eyebrows raised.

'I'd…um…like to help pay for it.'

The moment's silence was heavy. Sarah held his gaze. 'It's not necessary,' she said.

But she didn't sound convincing. About to argue, Rick was stopped by the continued eye contact. The intensity behind it.

'What Josh needs from you is something

money can't buy,' Sarah said softly. 'He needs something he's never had. A dad.'

Rick could feel every muscle in his body tense. 'I can't just morph into a dad, Sarah. I wouldn't have a clue where to begin.'

Sarah smiled. 'There's no "how to" manual.' She looked away. 'You just do your best for as long as you can.' She captured his gaze again. 'It might not even be for very long. Couldn't you at least give it a go?'

Part of Rick wanted to back away. As fast and as far as possible. He thought of Jet and his action to ward off bad voodoo and the idea of doing it himself had momentary appeal before being dismissed as inappropriate, not to mention immature.

There was another part of him that couldn't turn away from this. Not now. Something had changed today, thanks to both Sarah and the re-markable kid who was his son.

Maybe he'd grown up a little as well.

His nod was slow, but sure. He even managed a smile.

'I'll give a shot,' Rick said. 'I can't promise I'll be any good at it but I'll do my best.'

'That's all you need to do.' Sarah's smile lit up her eyes. She stood on tiptoe and put her arms around Rick's neck to hug him. 'Thank you.'

It was only a brief hug.

Weird the way he could still feel it, long after she had driven away into the night.

CHAPTER FIVE

JOSH was readmitted to hospital early on a Monday morning.

He received sedation to have the Hickman catheter inserted just under his collarbone and by lunchtime the intensive chemotherapy course to destroy his own bone marrow had begun.

The room in the bone-marrow transplant unit that was to become their world for the next few weeks felt remarkably like a prison to Sarah. It contained a bed for Josh and two armchairs of the kind that had controls to raise a footrest and tip back so they could be slept in comfortably. A small *en suite* bathroom a few steps away from the foot of the bed had a shower, toilet and hand-basin.

There were windows on the corridor side of the room, directly opposite an identical room that had yet to pull the curtains on their internal windows. On the outside wall was another window but the view was of another wing of the hospital. Dozens more windows that seemed like blank eyes staring back.

With a determinedly bright smile, Sarah turned away from the less than inspiring outlook. Josh was propped up on his pillows but still looked sleepy. The leg of a favourite soft toy poked out from under the covers beside him, one of the few personal items that gave this room a little bit of colour. The top buttons of his pyjama jacket were undone to reveal the dressing over the indwelling catheter. Close to that were rather complicated-looking connections that provided several ports. If necessary—and it probably would be—he could be infused with drugs and fluids and blood products all at the same time and there would still be access available to take blood samples.

Currently, Josh had sticky electrodes on his chest and wires that connected them to a cardiac monitor by his bed. A blood-pressure cuff was wrapped around his upper arm and inflated automatically at intervals to make re-cordings. A clip that measured the oxygen satu-ration in his blood completely covered the middle finger of his other hand. The steady beeping was a sound Sarah was well used to. It had been a comforting background, more than once, in the lonely hours of so many nights when she had been sitting alone beside a bed that looked just like this one. Wondering if Josh would still be alive in the morning.

Déjà vu of the worst kind. Pulling her back into something she would have done anything to be able to avoid. A sinking sensation that car-ried her on waves of heartbreak. Loneliness and frustration and unbearable sorrow.

A soft tap on the door advertised the arrival of a visitor and Sarah looked up to see the green gown and white mask that everyone who en-tered this room would have to wear from now on, including herself. It made everyone look the same and added an element that might end up being the worst aspect of this new admission so far. It felt like she and Josh had been sucked into something faceless. Impersonal.

Less caring.

She knew that was totally untrue. If anything, the opposite was the case but the dampening of an important sense in removing most of the features and facial expressions from the staff was hard to get used to. It made a person's eyes incredibly important as an avenue of communication so it was the first thing her gaze sought. This time, however, she recognised the new arrival even before he'd turned round as he manoeuvred something large and bulky into the room.

'Rick!'

His eyebrows rose. 'Is this a bad time to visit?'

'No…not at all. I just…' Hadn't expected the visit, that was all. Yes, he'd said he would get involved. Give being a father figure his best shot. But…

The voices had woken Josh. 'What's that?' he asked.

'Hey, buddy.' Rick's swift glance took in the bedside equipment. The monitors, the indwelling catheter and the bags of suspended fluid with their bright stickers to warn of the toxic drugs they contained. 'How're you doing?'

'I'm not being sick yet.'

'That's great.'

'What's that?'

'This?' Rick picked up the large object resting against his leg. 'It's a cork board.'

'You can't bring things like that in,' Sarah said. 'There's a risk of infection, especially from plant material, and that's—'

'Been decontaminated,' Rick interrupted. 'Sprayed to within an inch of its life. Like this other stuff.'

She hadn't noticed the box. Now she was as curious as Josh.

'That looks like the best spot.' Rick tilted the board and propped it against the wall beneath the window on the corridor side of the room. 'Easy viewing level when you're lying in bed, I reckon. What do you think, Josh?'

'I can see it all right.' Sarah could understand why Josh sounded dubious. A cork board? Was he supposed to draw pictures to pin on it like a five-year-old? Or wait for get-well cards from relatives he didn't have?

'Cool. Now…' Rick was opening the box. 'I've got something else in here.'

Josh's eyelids had started to droop but then he frowned and pushed them open again. 'What's that thing?"

'A camera. I know it looks a bit weird. It's an old-fashioned kind, not digital. Which is why I managed to acquire it. We used to use them in the old days. It's Polaroid and it takes instant pictures.' He aimed the camera at Josh and it clicked. Almost at once, a piece of white card began appearing from its base. 'This is the picture,' he told Josh. 'You have to wait for a minute or two for it to develop. See?'

He was beside the head of the bed now, holding the card for Josh to watch. Sarah watched them, feeling absurdly pleased that Rick had come to visit so early on and that Josh was looking interested. Too distracted to be thinking about anything else, in fact. She felt the same way. The fear and the loneliness and the sense of confinement was gone. Tucked away in some part of her brain that she had no need to access while Rick was there.

'Hey…that's *me*.' Josh sounded delighted.

'Sure is.' Rick glanced at Sarah, including her in the conversation. 'It's a picture of your first day in here. Tomorrow we can take another one. I thought you might like a kind of photo album on the wall so you can see all the milestones on the road to getting better.'

Josh turned to Sarah. 'You can take a picture of me throwing up.'

'Cool. Not.'

'There might be some pictures from home you could stick onto the board,' Rick suggested. 'To remind Josh of the good stuff he can look forward to when he gets out of here. Maybe even a picture of something extra-special that could be a reward.'

'A dog,' Josh said promptly. 'That's what I want. My own puppy.'

'Oh, Josh…you know we're not allowed to keep

pets in the apartment.' Sarah could feel the slide of an emotional roller-coaster. A moment ago she'd been blown away by the thought Rick had put into this gift. The promise of his involvement in saying *we* could take another picture tomorrow and every day after that. Now he was making her the bad guy here. Letting Josh reveal a dream that she had no hope of fulfilling even if everything else went perfectly.

Josh was not only looking awake right now, his eyes were shining and his lips were curved into a dreamy smile. Thinking about the puppy he'd wanted for ever.

A dog would be my friend, he'd told her once. *Then it wouldn't matter if I was too sick to go to school.*

'You might not live in that apartment for ever.'

Rick's gaze was on Sarah now and there was a question in his eyes that she could read remarkably clearly. Was it really a bad thing to let Josh dream about something that might help him get through the worst of this? Even if it didn't eventuate? Yes, part of Sarah wanted to respond. She'd always been honest with Josh. False hope wasn't necessarily better than no hope. Except...except that Josh was looking happier right now than she'd seen him look in ages. He wasn't counting down the hours until he started throwing up or found himself in unbearable pain. He was thinking about something that might actually make going through everything that was to come worthwhile. And it wasn't totally dishonest. It was highly likely they wouldn't have to live in that apartment for ever, especially if she could start working again.

'We could get a house,' Josh said happily. 'With a garden. Couldn't we, Sarah? One day?'

'Absolutely we could,' Sarah found herself saying. 'We'll find a picture of one we might like, shall we? And stick it on the board?'

'Yeah...' But Josh sounded sleepy again. His eyes drifted shut and he seemed to melt further into his pillows but he still had a smile tilting the corners of his mouth.

Rick pinned the Polaroid snap onto the corkboard. 'I'll show you how to use this camera,' he said to Sarah. 'Then you can take pictures when I'm not around. I'll show Josh how to use it tomorrow.'

'It was a wonderful idea, Rick. Thank you.'

'No worries.' Rick shrugged off the praise. It took only a few moments for him to demonstrate the workings of the camera. 'I've got a ton of the blank cards,' he told her. 'It all became redundant ages ago and ended up in my office for some reason. It's nice to have a use for it. And now…' the corners of his eyes crinkled as he smiled beneath the mask '…I've got to run. I've got a mountain of stuff to get through in the next couple of days so I can take some time off.'

'Oh…of course. When is your procedure scheduled for?'

'Wednesday, at the moment. Depends on how Josh goes with the prep.'

'Are you going to get knocked out?'

'No. I don't want a general anaesthetic.'

Sarah nodded. She had expected he wouldn't. 'What about the IV sedation? I think I'd go for a bucket of that.'

'They have offered me some jungle juice but I declined.' A flash of something like embarrassment showed on Rick's face. He had clearly been attracted by the prospect. 'It would mean I couldn't drive for twenty-four hours afterwards and I don't want to have to spend the night in here.'

'I could drive you home,' Sarah offered. 'And pick you up the next day.'

Rick didn't meet her eyes. 'I can cope with the local.'

He'd prefer not to have to, though, wouldn't he? Anyone would. 'Why make it worse for yourself than it has to be?' she asked carefully. 'Heaven knows, you're doing enough as it is. It's no big deal if I give you a ride home and pick you up the next morning.'

'You wouldn't want to leave Josh.'

'It wouldn't be for long. He'd be fine. I'd really like to…' Sarah held Rick's gaze. 'What you've done…are doing for Josh. It's really…'

The pleasure he had given. A chance to dream. Hope for a future.

It was beyond price. Beyond anything Sarah could find words to thank him for. She had to blink hard and turned slightly to look at Josh so that Rick wouldn't see how affected she was. She almost missed the shrugging movement Rick was making for the second time in that visit. She heard the rustle of his gown as he headed for the door.

'I said I'd give it my best shot,' he muttered. 'I'll let you know…about Wednesday.'

Rick headed for the intensive care unit. He had time to check on how young Simon was doing before he was due in Theatre for what would be a long and probably difficult surgery on a two-year-old girl who had a brain tumour with tentacles surrounding her spinal cord.

He was very pleased with the effect his brain wave about the old Polaroid camera had had. It had obviously distracted Josh from what was happening around him, albeit for only a short time, but, even better, he'd seen how Sarah had reacted. That initial surprise that he had actually come to visit. The quiet respect that he'd thought of a gift that could make a difference to how difficult this admission would be. There'd been that bristling at what she'd seen as stepping on her toes as a parent when he'd suggested that dreaming of a time when he could have his own dog wasn't so farfetched but then he'd seen… what?…acceptance? *Relief?*

No, that wasn't quite it but there'd been something. A connection. Maybe she believed now that he was prepared to try being a father figure for Josh and that she now had someone who was stepping up to share the burden. A partner.

Yes. Rick liked that idea. Sarah was more of a parent to Josh than he'd ever been but he had applied for a job-sharing arrangement and, so far, it was going well.

Better than he'd anticipated, in fact. Maybe this being a father thing wouldn't be so bad.

Josh was a good kid. He had looked pale and sick and had been through a fairly major procedure that morning. He was also confined to a small room where his only visitors had to be shrouded like alien beings and he was going to be in there for what must seem like an eternity to a nine-year-old, but he hadn't been whinging about any of it. He was a tough little nut. He'd wanted a photograph of him throwing up, for heaven's sake. Rick found himself grinning as he walked into Intensive Care.

Simon's parents were beside his bed. They both looked pale and were sitting very still. Their world had caved in on them, hadn't it? They were used to being in here now. Familiar with the machines and the new kind of care their son needed. Small things had become incredibly important but their focus was entirely on what was happening in here. World War Three could have broken out but they would still be totally focused. Watching for any signs that their precious child was going to survive and be all right.

Simon still lay like a small, reclining statue. Breathing on his own now but not showing any sign of coming out of the coma. Josh had been this pale but what a difference to be able to see the spark of life in a child's eyes. To be able to make them smile.

It wasn't that Rick had ever lacked any sympathy for the parents of his young patients. He would be going from this room to talk to the distraught family of the very sick toddler on his theatre list for this afternoon. He had seen too many parents suffering through this kind of experience. He'd seen the courage with which some of them faced inevitable failure and the agony of dealing with its aftermath. But he'd never felt quite like this. As though he knew the real level of pain it could cause because he could imagine what it would be like if it was Josh, lying here in Intensive Care. Or waiting in the ward to be taken for surgery that might save his life but could, quite possibly, end it.

He barely knew his own child but he knew that Josh had dreams. He wanted to go back to school. He wanted to live in a house that had a garden and a dog to play with. And Rick wanted him to have all those things. The desire to make it happen was sudden and fierce and almost threatened to overwhelm him.

He had to clear his throat as he looked up from reviewing Simon's chart.

'The intracranial pressure is coming down,' he told Simon's parents.

'That's good, isn't it?'

'Of course it is, honey,' the father said.

Simon's mother looked like she was holding her breath, too frightened to accept good news unless it could be trusted.

'It's very good,' Rick told her. 'Along with everything else that's settling down, it means that Simon's condition is stable. We'll be able to send him to Theatre to have his leg dealt with properly.'

'And will he wake up? After that?'

'I don't know,' Rick had to admit. 'I'm sorry, but I can't give you any definite time when that might happen. It's a matter of continuing to look after him and waiting to see what happens as the swelling keeps going down.'

'But it's a step in the right direction, isn't it?'

Simon's father had covered his eyes with his hand. He gave a huge sniff and his wife reached out to hold his other hand. Then they smiled at each other and Rick could actually feel the strength being passed from one to the other.

They were a partnership. They could help each other get through this and because they had each other, they were far more likely to cope. Whatever happened.

He wanted it to be like that for him and Sarah. A partnership that really meant something. A support that would get her through whatever was coming. It gave him a good feeling, imagining himself in that supportive role. Being her rock. A hero, even. And who knew? It might end up being one of the most worthwhile things he would do in his life.

He was going to give it his best shot, that was for sure. For both Josh and Sarah.

The combination of a heavy drug regime and the radiotherapy were taking their toll on Josh.

By Wednesday he was running a temperature

and his platelet count was so low he'd needed a blood transfusion. His joints hurt enough to need some serious pain relief and the nausea and vomiting were only just under control.

He was miserable.

'Katie's on duty today. She's your favourite nurse, isn't she?'

The assent was reluctant.

'Do you want to look at the book Rick brought yesterday? The one about dogs?'

Josh said nothing. His eyes looked blank, as though nothing mattered any more. Sarah covered up her need to blink and swallow back the tears by reaching for the *Encyclopaedia of Dogs* that Rick had apparently found in the well-stocked hospital bookshop. She edged her chair even closer to Josh's bed and laid the book where he could see it, flicking through the pages and showing him pictures.

'Look at that! It's an Irish wolfhound. It's twice the size you are, short stuff. Imagine how much it would need to eat. I think something a bit smaller would be better, don't you?'

Josh gave a half-hearted shrug that reminded her rather strongly of the way Rick had reacted to praise the other day.

'It's Wednesday today,' she said, after a moment's silence. 'Rick's going to have his bone marrow collected this afternoon. Do you think he'll be as brave as you are with that kind of thing?'

That got a reaction. A look of disgust almost. ''Course he will.'

Was there an element of hero-worship in there already? It wouldn't surprise her in the least. Rick had appeared in Josh's life like a thunderbolt. Larger than life. Tall and handsome and clever. He lived in what would have to be a small boy's paradise with a constant live action show of trucks and ships and machinery doing important things. He had taken Josh for a ride on his motorbike. He'd become a regular visitor to this room and often arrived with a surprise. Like the camera and the book about dogs.

Was it a bad thing, that Josh might see his father as the new sun in his universe? It certainly added a very new dimension to his life. The visits were something to look forward to in an otherwise bleak environment and the new development of having a father who seemed to care about him was…absolute magic.

As long as Rick kept up his promise of involvement. Sarah didn't want to contemplate the consequences if he changed his mind and disappeared from Josh's life for whatever reason. Not that he was showing any sign of regretting his choice. He'd be taking the next step in a matter of hours, in fact. Going through what would probably be a painful and unpleasant medical procedure.

'You haven't forgotten that I'll be out for a while later? When I drive Rick home?'

Josh stared at her, that frightening blankness still in his face.

'It won't be for long. And Katie's going to stay in here to keep you company. That's OK, isn't it?'

The telltale wobble of a bottom lip made her heart sink like a stone. She couldn't leave him if it was going to cause further distress but she had promised Rick and she didn't want to let *him* down either. What was she going to do?

Trying to think, Sarah's gaze went back to the book lying on the bed cover. She turned a random number of pages.

'Good grief, look at that. Looks like a rat with a wig on, doesn't it?'

Josh barely glanced at the photograph of the hairless Chinese crested dog. Sarah's level of desperation increased.

'I might see that other dog again when I drive Rick home,' she said. 'You know, the one that was outside the coffee shop?'

That did it. The spark of interest made Josh's face come to life. Sarah's heart gave a painful squeeze.

'What will you do if you see it?'

Uh-oh... She was getting into dangerous territory here but she couldn't bear to see that blank look return.

'If it doesn't have someone looking after it, it might be lost. Or abandoned or something.'

Josh nodded. 'It would need someone to take it home, then, wouldn't it?'

'I guess.' Sarah mentally crossed her fingers, hoping that she might see the dog wearing a collar and lead. Being walked by a responsible dog owner.

'So you'll look out for it?'

'Yes.'

'When are you going?'

He actually wanted her to go now. If nothing else, it had solved her most immediate dilemma. 'Not till this afternoon. You'll be asleep, I expect.'

He was looking ready to sleep again now. Struggling to keep his eyes open. 'But you'll wake me up when you get back? And tell me?'

'Absolutely.'

Josh gave a big sigh and his eyes drifted shut. 'That's good,' he mumbled.

'I didn't see it.'

'See what?'

'The dog.'

'What dog?' Rick wanted to make that crease on Sarah's forehead disappear but he had no idea what she was talking about. It probably had something to do with the dramatic increase in his level of pain, having had his long frame folded into her small car for what seemed like a long time now. Or maybe his brain was fuzzy due to the after-effects of the IV sedation. No wonder you weren't allowed to drive for a while.

'That scruffy mutt we saw outside the coffee shop that day. Josh is worried about it. He wanted me to keep an eye out and rescue it if I saw it wandering around.'

'And take it to the pound?'

Sarah's laugh was a little hollow. 'I think he'd prefer me to take it home.'

It was Rick's turn to frown now. 'Might be just as well you didn't see it, then.'

'Yeah...I guess.'

'What, you think you could cope with having an illegal hound in your apartment as well as having Josh in hospital?'

'No, of course not. It's just...'

'What?' Rick had to suppress an urge to reach out and touch Sarah to encourage her to keep talking. He smiled at her instead, which seemed to do the trick.

'Well…he was so unhappy today. Sick and sore and miserable, and I've never seen him look quite like that. Blank, you know? Like he would just give up on everything if he was given half a chance. But when I mentioned the dog, he…came alive again. It was…it was…' Sarah pressed her lips together and squeezed her eyes shut.

Rick did touch her this time. Just a friendly squeeze on the arm still holding the steering-wheel.

'I get it,' he said. 'Hey, I'll keep an eye out for it myself. I often go past there, on my way to the hamburger shop.'

'Oh…that reminds me. Have you got something for your dinner?'

'I'm not exactly hungry. Might just take some of the nice painkillers they've given me and wash them down with a shot of something tastier than water.'

Sarah's eyes darkened with sympathy. 'Poor you. Um…do you need a hand getting up the steps?'

He didn't, of course. Sure, he was pretty sore but it wasn't about to incapacitate him. But he rather liked the way she was looking at him right now. As though how he felt mattered enough for her to be sharing his pain. Jet would have given him a thump on his arm and told him to 'harden up, man'.

'That would be nice,' he heard himself saying in a voice small enough to make him very glad Jet wasn't around to overhear. 'If you've got the time, that is. You must be wanting to get back to Josh.'

'He's fine. He had a big dose of painkillers himself just before I left and went out like a light. His nurse thought he'd be asleep for a good few hours.'

She put her arm around Rick when he started climbing the steps and that felt so nice he probably went a lot slower than he actually needed to go. And then they were inside and there was no reason for her to stay any longer but Rick didn't want her to leave just yet.

'Can I make you a cup of tea or something?'

Sarah hesitated, gave Rick a long glance and then took a deep breath. 'Why don't I make one for both of us? That way I can make sure you feel OK after you have your pills. I don't want to rush away and have you fall over and hit your head or something.'

They both went into the kitchen. Sarah boiled the jug and found some mugs while Rick threw down a couple of pills with a shot of whisky. He couldn't help noticing the glance she threw at him.

'Don't worry, I'm not about to down the whole bottle. The faster these pills work the quicker I'll get to sleep. A good night and I'll be as right as rain by the morning.'

'If you say so.' Sarah took the steaming mugs to the low table near the chairs.

Rick lowered himself very carefully.

'Is it really bad?'

He shrugged. 'Feels a bit like I came off my bike and landed on my bum.'

Her lips twitched. 'On a scale of zero to ten? Zero being—'

Rick laughed. 'You're such a nurse. I'm fine. Let's stop talking about it. Tell me something about you instead.'

'Like what?'

Like what, indeed?

He could ask about her childhood but that would inevitably mean talking about her sister and Rick would end up feeling guilty. He didn't want to have to think about how his irresponsibility might have derailed a young woman's life.

He was making up for it now, wasn't he? Trying to, anyway.

He could ask about her career but that would mean talking about medicine. Work. The experience of being on the patient's side of the equation was a little too fresh to make that appealing. It would be nice to forget about hospitals for a while.

What did that leave?

Sarah herself. In the present time. Yes…that was definitely what he'd like to talk about. If he could think up a question. It seemed oddly difficult to catch what was inside his head and make it come out in words.

'How bold are you?'

'Sorry?' Sarah came very close to slopping her drink all over her clothing.

'I meant how *old* are you?'

'Twenty-seven.'

'And how long have you been…? How long…' Rick narrowed his eyes to help him concentrate '…with Josh?'

Sarah understood. 'Coming up to three years now. He was six when the accident happened and Lucy was killed.'

Oops. The sister. How could he divert the topic?

'Mmm. The motorbike.' No. That wasn't a good direction. 'Boyfriend,' Rick muttered experimentally. That seemed to be an improvement. Relief made him smile at Sarah. 'Have you got a boyfriend?'

'No.' The word was clipped.

Rick looked away. He didn't want to be caught looking pleased about that or anything. He eyed the mug of tea. He'd rather have another shot of whisky but that probably wouldn't be a good idea. He was feeling pleasantly numb around the edges already. The pain was rapidly becoming very distant.

'I did,' Sarah said into the growing silence. 'He took off after Josh arrived. He wasn't about to include someone else's kid in his life.'

'Creep,' Rick said helpfully.

'Not really. It's a big ask.'

It wouldn't be for *him*, though, would it? He liked Josh. A lot. Which was good because he was *his* kid after all. Weird how proud that was making him feel right now. Rick could feel himself smiling broadly.

'What's funny?' Sarah had an odd note in her voice. It also sounded as if it was coming from rather a long way away. 'Rick…are you feeling all right?'

'I'm fun.'

'Hmm. Maybe you should go to bed.'

'Mmm.' This was the best idea yet. He kept smiling at Sarah. 'Come with me?'

'Oh...*God*,' Sarah muttered. She stood up, helped Rick to his feet and put a firm arm around his waist. 'Come on. You need to sleep.'

Rick's feet felt like dead weights but he could walk just fine. Until he got to the stairs leading to the mezzanine level where his bed was. Sarah turned him round after his attempt at the first step nearly had them both on the floor.

'Couch,' she said. 'I'll get a pillow and some blankets. You're not safe with stairs.'

She was right. Rick was still with it enough to be able to keep himself safe. He even managed to pull his shoes off and lie down on the couch by the time she returned.

Sarah put a glass of water and his mobile phone on the table nearby. She covered him with the duvet from his bed and then bent down to ease a pillow under his head.

'You're a wonderful woman, Sarah,' he said,

pleased at how clearly the words came out. Lying down was good.

'Are you going to be all right on your own, do you think?'

'Just need to catch a few zeds. I'm fine. You go.'

She hesitated.

'The phone's there.' Rick flapped a hand. 'I'll call you if I need rescue, OK? I'm not totally away with the fairies. Just…just…' He let himself float for a moment. 'Just happy.'

'Hmm.' It sounded like Sarah was smiling. 'I can see that. I guess the pills are at maximum effect by now. They'll wear off while you sleep.'

'Ni'-night.'

'Sleep well, Rick. You're a hero.'

He opened one eye. 'Do I get a goodnight kiss, then?'

Sarah shook her head as she gave a huff of laughter. 'You're a rogue,' she told him.

But then she bent and gave him a swift, soft kiss on his lips. She was standing again before he could even think of making his arms move to catch her.

'I'll see you in the morning,' she said. 'Sleep tight.'

It didn't matter that he hadn't been able to catch and hold Sarah. He could imagine exactly what it would have been like. And what might have happened if her lips had stayed in contact with his a little longer.

The pleasant fuzziness of the painkillers morphed into something so delicious that Rick could only heave a sigh of pure contentment and go with it. To paradise.

He had no idea how long Sarah sat watching him and he didn't hear a thing when she finally slipped away, closing the door softly behind her.

CHAPTER SIX

R<small>ICK'S</small> text message to Sarah the next day sounded faintly embarrassed.

Max back in town, it said. *No need to collect me.*

Sarah wouldn't have been surprised if Rick had found an excuse not to visit Josh. After the twenty-four-hour stand-down period he would have some catching up to do on his patients and by the time he'd been on his feet that long, he might well be sore enough to want to head straight home again. It was to his credit that he turned up late that afternoon.

He did, however, avoid direct eye contact with Sarah. And he muttered an apology about 'last night' before he got close enough to Josh's bed to be overheard.

'No worries,' Sarah said calmly. 'You were… um…happy.'

'High as a kite, more like.' His tone was rueful. 'I should have stuck to the local.'

Sarah turned back to the window. She could understand him feeling embarrassed about how friendly he'd been but he didn't have to rub it in. Unless, of course, he wanted her to be absolutely sure he saw her as Josh's aunt-cum-mother and nothing else.

Well…fine. She saw him as nothing more than Josh's father. Inappropriate words or touches on his part that might have occurred as the result of close proximity and inhibitions being stifled by medication could be forgiven and forgotten. Along with that oddly protective urge she'd experienced that had led her to sit and watch over him last night. And the way she'd unconsciously found herself touching her own lips softly, more than once, as though reliving that brief kiss.

At least Josh wasn't picking up on any weird vibe.

'Does your bum hurt?' he asked Rick.

'Kind of...you know.'

Josh did know. He was eyeing Rick with new respect. He nodded importantly and, with a visible effort, straightened up against his pillows. A deliberate imitation of Rick's solid stance?

They were watching each other. Man and boy. Both had to be thinking about the physical discomfort of a procedure they had both endured recently. Sarah could almost feel the way their mutual respect grew. She saw the smile of quiet pride on Josh's exhausted face and the way the creases around Rick's eyes deepened as he returned it. She could feel the connection then. Still new and nebulous but definitely there, and her own lips curved into a slightly wobbly smile beneath her mask.

Oh, yes... She could forgive Rick anything. Even the stirring of things far better left to lie still that his request for a goodnight kiss had achieved. This was more than simply fronting up and trying to act like a father. There was a growing bond that went far deeper than going through the motions. Right now, Rick and Josh might both be proud of themselves but, far more significantly, they were also proud of each other.

Rick made that casual shrugging gesture she was coming to recognise as shying away from being praised. It suggested an appealing modesty. 'Take any photographs today?' he asked Josh.

'Yeah.' Josh managed a faint grin. 'Me throwing up. See?'

Rick dutifully took note of the new addition to the cork board. It wasn't graphic—just Josh with his face attached to the rim of a vomit container, but he'd been happy and maybe he'd been right. The picture deserved a slot in the visual diary. Maybe later they would look back and be able to see how long ago it had been since he'd felt so awful.

Sarah wasn't feeling so great herself. Josh had still been asleep when she'd finally come back last night after her vigil over Rick but she'd been unable to sleep. Now, when she moved to go and sit down on one of the chairs, she had to catch the rail at the end of the bed to steady herself.

How on earth had Rick managed to catch her elbow so fast?

'Are you all right?'

Oh…Lord. That expression in those dark eyes threatened to undo her completely. When had somebody last demonstrated real concern for *her*? When had anybody *ever* looked at her quite like that? Stupidly, it made her want to cry.

'Are you going to throw up?' Josh asked with interest.

'No…' But Sarah was still caught by Rick's gaze. 'I mean, yes. I'm all right. I'm fine. Just…a bit tired, I guess.'

'How much have you had to eat today?'

'Only lunch so far.'

'You didn't eat your lunch,' Josh reminded her. He yawned. 'It came while I was throwing up, remember? You said it didn't look so good after all.'

Rick was frowning. 'And you didn't have breakfast?'

'I had coffee.'

'And last night? After you got back from tucking me in?' At least he could sound casual about it now. 'Did you have a proper dinner?'

What would he say if she told him it had been far too late to visit the cafeteria because she'd sat watching him sleep for so long? That would bring the embarrassment back with a vengeance, wouldn't it? She didn't want to do that.

Rick shook his head. 'Ellie's coming in to say hi soon. You should both go out and get some food. There's a nice bistro only a block or so away from here. They do great pasta.'

Josh spoke with his eyes shut. 'Is Ellie coming to visit *me*?'

'She won't be allowed in here,' Sarah said apologetically. 'Sorry, Josh, but there's a strict limit on who gets in to visit you. At the moment it's just me and Rick and your doctors and nurses.'

'Cos you're my mum now,' Josh mumbled.

'That's right, short stuff.'

'And Rick's my dad.'

Sarah's hesitation was imperceptible. She didn't dare look at Rick. She bent down and kissed Josh's head instead. 'Yeah…'

Josh made a very sleepy sound of approval. When Sarah straightened, she saw the door opening to admit a nurse who was coming in to do the vital-sign monitoring that was due. She also saw Rick slipping out. And beyond him, as he stripped off the mask and gown, she could see Ellie, looking anxious.

The cringe factor was still there.

Every time he caught direct eye contact with Sarah, Rick had the very uncomfortable feeling that she might be able to see remnants of those incredible, drug-fuelled dreams he'd had about her last night.

He had been fairly confident this morning that he could remember where reality had left off and fantasy had taken over, but what if that was merely wishful thinking on his part? What if it hadn't been as chaste a kiss as he thought? Had he actually tasted the sweet scent of her mouth? Felt the slide of her tongue driving him into a passion that had been as overwhelming as it had been unrecognisable?

If so, either Sarah had been totally unmoved by the experience or she was an extremely good actress. Even now, watching her greet Ellie, catch up on news of the honeymoon and relay an update on Josh, he couldn't detect any tension. Or any of those secret female, telepathic-type messages about something personal that needed private analysis and resolution.

Ellie was apologising again for having been out of the country when her friend had needed support.

'We've been fine,' Sarah assured her. 'Rick's been absolutely wonderful.'

Ellie's eyes widened.

So did Rick's. His chest might have puffed out just a little as well. He shrugged it off.

'Haven't done much,' he muttered. 'It's my kid in there, after all.'

But Ellie was biting her lip and smiling at the same time. She hugged Sarah. Then she stood on tiptoe and threw her arms around Rick's neck, hugging him tightly.

'I knew you'd end up being a hero,' she whispered. 'Thank you.'

He'd 'ended up' being a hero? She was thanking him? Sarah's expression was softened by heartfelt gratitude as well. As though he'd done something they'd wanted badly but hadn't really expected him to do.

Fair enough. He hadn't exactly behaved very well when first confronted by the possibility of Josh being his son, had he? But he hadn't known anything about these people back then. Was it really such a short time ago? They were part of his life now. Important. Special.

Oh…hell. These two women looked like they were about to start crying. He didn't want any more gratitude or talk about heroics. He was no hero. If he hadn't been so irresponsible and uncaring in the first place, none of this would be happening to any of them. Including the innocent kid in the room right beside them who was suffering most.

This was *his* fault. All of it.

'Sarah's starving,' he informed Ellie. 'She

hasn't eaten all day and she was so wobbly in there she almost fell over. I thought you could take her to that nice bistro down the road and fill her up with pasta or something.'

'Oh...' Ellie looked stricken. 'Max is looking after Mattie but he's covering for someone in ED for a few hours yet.' Her glance at Sarah was very apologetic. It became inspired when it returned to Rick.

'*You* could take her,' Ellie said.

'It's OK,' Sarah said hurriedly. 'I can get something from the cafeteria. That way I can get back to Josh faster.'

The odd combination of relief and disappointment Rick was experiencing got interrupted by the door of Josh's room opening. His nurse, Katie, poked her head out.

'Josh wants a rerun of his Harry Potter DVD and I haven't seen all of it so I'm going to stay with him. Why don't you have a good break, Sarah? A nice meal and a shower and so on. Do you good.'

'But—'

'I've got your mobile number. I'll ring if Josh needs you.'

Katie disappeared back into the room. They could all see the screen of the television set that angled down from the ceiling in the corner of the room. They could also see Josh, his eyes only half-open but already glued to the images of his favourite movie.

There was a moment's silence in the corridor as Rick struggled to eradicate the last of that cringe factor. But, suddenly, he stopped trying. Maybe it was a good thing. A kind of penance. He could learn from it and maybe even continue the process of finally growing up that seemed to have started under Sarah's orders.

'I can recommend the ravioli,' he said, raising his eyebrows and letting a smile curve one side of his mouth. 'How 'bout it? My treat… I owe you a thank-you for your kind taxi service yesterday.'

Sarah looked back through the window. There must be a scary scene happening judging by the wide eyes of both Josh and Katie and the way they were holding hands. She looked at Ellie, who nodded with firm encouragement.

'Go on,' she urged. 'A break from here is exactly what you need. I know I'm a much better mum when I've had a bit of a break from Mattie. Speaking of whom…'

'You go,' Sarah told her. 'I'll call you tomorrow and…' she flicked a glance at Rick '…tell you whether the ravioli lives up to its reputation.'

Sarah had known this might be awkward.

She also knew that unless they could get past it, it might grow into something a lot worse than mild embarrassment. If Rick started to avoid her, he would, by default, be avoiding Josh and she couldn't let that happen.

Not now, with that new bond developing. Having a father he could be proud of—who was proud of *him*—had to be the best gift Josh could ever receive. Whatever it took, she had to make sure he didn't lose that gift or have its value undermined in some way. Any private feelings she might have in the matter of including Rick in their lives were irrelevant. Or had to become so in a hurry.

So she did her best to chatter brightly as they walked the short distance to the bistro. About Josh, of course, and the happenings of the day.

'He's doing pretty well, all things considered,' she was saying as they reached their destination. 'Totally exhausted but Mike says that's only to be expected. He thinks we're on track to do the transplant tomorrow. Or the next day.' She couldn't help the tiny gulp that punctuated the prediction.

'Nervous about it?' Rick's hand was on her elbow as he steered her through the door into a small, dimly lit establishment, made cheerful by its warmth and the tempting smell of hot food.

'Yes. He ran through the list of things they'd be watching for while the transfusion happens. Fever and chills and hives and chest pain and so on. It's a big deal. I'm not sure I can hold my breath for that long.'

She stopped talking as they were shown to a table tucked into the corner of the room, with two old wooden chairs on the available sides. It had a checked cloth and a slim candle stuck in an old, misshapen wine bottle that carried the dribbles of wax from years of service.

Sarah had to smile. 'This takes me back to my student days. I didn't think places like this existed any more.'

Tables around them were rapidly filling up.

'We'd better order soon or we might end up being here for a while.' Rick signalled the young waitress.

Sarah ordered a wild mushroom ravioli with roasted red pepper sauce. Rick chose the individual ravioli lasagne.

'Garlic bread?' The waitress flicked a lighter and leaned in to light their candle.

'Please.'

'Anything to drink? Do you want the wine list?'

Sarah caught Rick's questioning glance. 'Why not?' she decided aloud. A glass of wine would be a rare treat these days.

'I think I'd better stick to water,' Rick said

when Sarah had made her choice. His grin was endearingly self-deprecating. 'After last night, I mean.'

Sarah sighed but smiled at the same time. 'Don't make such a big deal out of it, Rick. It was kind of cute, really—asking for a goodnight kiss.'

She looked up and then wished she hadn't because she got caught. Candlelight flickered and Rick's eyes were very dark and watchful. The echo of the last word she'd spoken seemed to dance in the space between them and all she could think about for a moment was kissing.

Kissing Rick.

'Hardly a grown-up thing to do,' he said softly.

Good heavens... Her angry words that day she'd left Josh on his doorstep must have really hit home.

'Just as well I'm used to boy stuff, then,' she said lightly. 'Let's forget it.'

'OK.' But Rick still seemed on edge. 'Guess I'll have to add it to the list of things to do with you that I'm not so proud of.'

'A whole list?' Sarah was very thankful that her wine had arrived. A large first mouthful on her very empty stomach was having an instant effect in relaxing her. 'Oh, come on…you're doing something you have every right to feel *very* proud of.'

'Being a donor?' Rick was toying with his water glass. Running his thumb up the side to wipe off condensation the iced liquid had caused. Sarah couldn't take her eyes off the movement. His long, surgeon's fingers. The delicate, intense touch.

'Has it occurred to you that it's actually my fault that Josh is going through this whole business?'

'*What*?' Sarah shifted her gaze from his hands to his face. 'Don't be daft. You can hardly take the blame for Josh getting sick.'

'But I can for him being here at all. For the way I treated your sister.' Rick looked away. 'All I can say in my defence is that it was a bad time. Self-destruction seemed like the only escape route I could find.'

'I know.' Seemingly of its own volition, her hand stretched across the table to touch Rick's. His skin felt more than alive. It tingled and burned under her fingers and she had to pull her hand back in case it showed. 'Ellie told me about your friend Matt. I'm sorry. It must have been a terrible time for all of you.'

Rick merely nodded. He took a gulp of his water and Sarah followed his example and picked up her wine glass again.

Oh…help. This was a vast topic and not one Sarah had expected Rick to bring up. She didn't want him feeling guilty, though. Or feeling like he owed Josh something just because he was sick. She wanted Josh to have a father he could look up to and love. Who would love him back with the kind of unconditional love that could only be tainted by things like guilt or pity.

She took another mouthful of the wine, set her glass down again and then spoke slowly and carefully.

'Lucy was a big girl. It was her choice to sleep with you, Rick. She was hardly behaving that well herself, was she, if she jumped into bed with someone else fast enough to assume the baby was his when she found out she was pregnant.'

'She really didn't think it was me?'

'Apparently not.' Should she tell Rick about what she'd said to Josh? About his father riding a motorbike and being so handsome? Sarah swallowed hard. 'She never said anything to me about you. I had no idea you even existed.' She couldn't help letting her gaze rest on his face for a moment and she certainly couldn't stop the smile that tugged at her lips. 'Seems weird now.'

Why was that? With a sinking sensation, Sarah realised that it was because he had already made such an impact on her life that she would always be aware of him in some way. And she'd as much as told him so.

But Rick only made a grunting sound that could have been agreement. Thankfully, he seemed to have missed the implication. Except he *was* frowning.

Sarah held her breath, waiting for him to speak.

'Do you think it wrecked her life?' he asked abruptly. 'Getting pregnant?'

Sarah was given time to consider her response by the arrival of their meals. The food was the most delicious she'd tasted in a very long time and she had to eat a couple of mouthfuls despite being aware of Rick waiting anxiously for her to speak.

'Sorry. I was starving.'

'No worries. I probably shouldn't be asking you anyway. It's just…I've been thinking about it, that's all.'

'Of course you have.' Sarah rested her fork on her plate and gave him her full attention. 'Being pregnant didn't wreck Lucy's life. It changed it but I think she was happier for that change.'

'Why?'

'She was a country girl at heart. We grew up in a small town and she was quite intimidated by the city. I think she felt pretty lost. Lonely, even.'

'She must have gone through hell, then, finding she was pregnant and wondering what to do.'

'She was tough.' Sarah's smile was fond. 'She coped. She didn't even tell me until well down the track. And neither of us told our mother.'

'Why not?'

'She had a very strict moral code. She raised us on her own after Dad died and I don't think she found that much joy in the process. Her church was more important than anything. When she eventually found out, she never spoke to Lucy again.'

'God…*families*…'

Sarah ignored the undercurrent of his tone.

'When Josh was born Luce fell in love with him and he was all that mattered. She wasn't going to let anyone take him away from her and that meant never involving the father. He was her family. Her future. When Mum died, she left me her house. I was going to sell it and give Luce the money but she decided that being out in the country would be a good place to raise Josh. She was so excited about it.' Sarah took a deep breath. 'You didn't wreck her life, Rick. You gave her a dream. Like…like telling Josh that he could have a dog one day, you know? It's kind of like hope that the perfect life is there, just waiting for you. And maybe…'

She stopped talking, appalled at what she had been about to say. That maybe Lucy had been dreaming of finding a father for Josh who would be just like Rick. She choked back both the words and the sentiments they represented. Absurdly, she found herself close to tears. She tried to pick up her fork but her hand was shaking so she dropped it with a clatter and reached for her wineglass again.

She knew she should say more but how could she without revealing far too much about the way she was reacting to Rick? She didn't want to talk any more about Lucy right now either.

Why is that? an insistent voice in her head queried. *Because you don't want the ghost of your sister standing between you and this man?*

Sarah drained her glass and made of a show of returning her attention to her food. Rick was watching her very intently but he didn't say anything other than offering her another glass of wine, which she refused.

In fact, neither of said very much for the rest of the meal or the walk back to Queen Mary's, and Sarah had no idea whether she'd been successful in trying to abort the guilt trip Rick had embarked on.

She was making a map of a rather similar kind of journey herself. Along the lines of cashing in on a fantasy Lucy could no longer even dream about. Good heavens, wasn't being attracted to a man her own sister had slept with unacceptable enough all by itself?

Of course it was. This had to stop.

'Let me know when they schedule the transplant,' Rick said as they reached the main doors of the hospital. 'I'd like to be there.'

Sarah nodded. 'I will. Thanks.'

'What for?'

'Oh...the meal. Being here...' Being *you*, she couldn't help adding silently. 'You know...'

Rick had that watchful look again. 'Maybe it should be *me* thanking you.'

Sarah blinked. 'What for?'

'Oh…I don't know. Making me grow up, perhaps? Being…' He hesitated for a heartbeat. 'Are we friends yet, Sarah?'

'I think so,' she said gravely. But then she smiled. 'Don't grow up completely. Keep a bit of that boy stuff.'

'What, like asking for a goodnight kiss?'

It was a light-hearted comment. They were standing right in front of the entranceway. Any moment now and Sarah would go inside and back to the bone-marrow transplant unit. Rick would head for the car park and home. All they needed to do was share a smile and any embarrassment from last night would evaporate for ever and they could part on a new level of friendship.

The smile was there already. The intention to leave at that was also there. So why on earth did she stay exactly where she was?

'I'm the one who had the wine,' she heard herself saying. 'I think it's my turn to ask.'

She didn't have to.

'Fair enough.' Rick was smiling as he dipped his head and touched her lips with his own.

It was a brief kiss. The kind that friends could exchange. There was nothing more in its length or pressure than the token gesture she had given Rick last night but it was different. Very, very different.

Dangerous.

The electric sensation of touching his hand with hers had nothing on this contact of their lips.

Sarah was playing with fire here, and she knew it was wrong. She could blame it on exhaustion, or the wine, or stress, or the fact that her hormones were in flood after the longest drought, but no excuse was going to make it any less wrong.

Summoning every ounce of strength she possessed, Sarah broke the contact almost the instant it had happened and turned away.

'See?' Her tone was so light it floated. 'No big deal. Goodnight, Rick.'

The doors slid open with admirable swiftness.

She knew Rick was still standing there but no way was she going to risk a backward glance.

It wasn't going to happen, she told herself fiercely, increasing her speed. She wasn't going to allow it to happen.

Sarah could not, *would* not, fall in love with Rick Wilson.

He was Josh's father.

Quite possibly the most important person right now in a small boy's life.

A small boy she loved with all her heart.

A life that was hanging in the balance.

CHAPTER SEVEN

THE tension in that small room could have been cut with a knife.

'Drip, drip, drip,' Josh said, looking up at the bag of dark, red fluid hanging above his head. 'It looks like blood.'

'It's better than blood,' Mike told his young patient. 'It's the stuff that *makes* blood.'

'How's it going to get inside my bones?'

'Through the blood vessels. The same way the new blood gets out.'

'How does it know to stay in there? Why doesn't it just keeping floating round and round?'

'It's smart.'

Mike was watching Josh intently for any sign of an adverse reaction to the transfusion. The boy lay with only his pyjama pants on. His chest was bare, partly so they could watch for the beginnings of any rash and also because it was well plastered with electrodes for the continuous ECG monitoring every beat of his heart. Blood pressure was being recorded automatically every few minutes and Josh's favourite nurse, Katie, was standing with a clipboard, noting down everything that was being tracked.

Sarah was there too, of course. She was sitting beside the bed but Josh had refused to have his hand held.

'I'm not a baby,' he'd said. 'And it doesn't even hurt.'

Rick was standing beside the window. A part of this procedure but outside the inner circle with nothing to do but watch. And feel the atmosphere pressing in on him. Was this tension only due to the importance of this procedure going well?

Not for him.

He'd been over and over it in his head ever since Sarah had walked through those doors last night but he was no closer to making sense of any of it.

What the hell had been going on last night?

Things had been going so well. That bistro was one of his favourite places with its unpretentious, laid-back atmosphere. Kind of casual but intimate at the same time. The food had been up to its usual standard and he'd found himself thoroughly enjoying the company. Especially when Sarah had seemed intent on making him feel better about the notion that had been haunting him. That he might have completely derailed her sister's life by being the cause of an unwanted pregnancy.

She'd almost been telling him he'd made her life better, for God's sake. That he'd given Lucy a whole new direction. A *dream*… And then she'd clammed up and had had that look of struggling *not* to say what was on the tip of her tongue.

He'd seen that look before, he'd realised last night, sitting at his window watching a night shift in action on the wharf and puzzled by the mixed signals he seemed to have been given. Right back when they'd first met at the wedding. He'd asked her about her trip to the States. About searching for a possible donor for Josh. She'd known she was talking to that person right then but she'd promised not to say anything, hadn't she, so she'd buttoned her lip.

What did that have to do with what she'd been saying about Lucy? She'd dreamed of a family. Raising her kid in the country and having a dog. The perfect life. Except it hadn't been, had it, because her precious son had been missing something important. A father.

Him.

Whatever she'd said, there was still blame to be found. He'd changed the whole direction of her sister's life and then abandoned her because it had meant nothing to him. Left her with a child and a dream that was never fulfilled. Of course she would blame him, and fair enough.

He could handle that but he'd thought they'd got past it and the beginnings of a real friendship were there. She'd forgiven him for the stupid, drug-induced pass he'd made at her. *No big deal*, she'd said.

She'd even kissed him to prove it.

Except it *had* been a big deal. For him. That

fleeting contact of her lips... Being close enough to smell her scent and feel the warmth of her breath... Oh, *man*...

It was still there in the room. That kiss. Like an elephant. Sarah probably didn't even see it. Partly because her attention was entirely on Josh but also because it had meant nothing to her.

Was this karma? He'd slept with her sister and the repercussions were still crashing into his life like a tidal wave. His attraction to Sarah was just part of it and the whole picture was laced with emotion that pulsed like a life force. A network of vessels like the ones inside Josh that *his* bone marrow was now a part of. Things were too mingled to separate. Him and Josh. Him and Sarah. It was...

Confusing, that was what it was.

'Why doesn't my dad come and visit me any more?'

'He *does*. Every day.'

The hesitation was telling. So was the plaintive note in Josh's voice. 'Not so much.'

Sarah's hands stilled in her task of sifting through DVDs to try and find something that might interest a bored child. It was true. Ever since the transplant had happened, the number of times per day that Rick came in to see them had dropped dramatically. OK, it had only been a few days but the hope that only she was noticing was something she could no longer cling to.

It was disturbing to say the least.

Did Rick feel like his duty was done now? The donation of bone marrow had been made and apparently accepted by Josh's body so far, with no sign of rejection issues. It was probably too early to stop worrying about the onset of graft versus host disease. Or was it? She needed to ask Mike about that when he came in on his rounds. She could ask Rick but the routine visit from Josh's consultant was more likely to occur first. Rick seemed to be leaving it later and later in his day to pop in and the visits seemed to be getting shorter.

Less…personal.

Or maybe that was only from her point of view

because Rick was so focused on Josh when he *was* in the room. The man and boy seemed to be getting closer and more comfortable with each other every day. She felt like she was being shut out. Rick was perfectly polite and friendly to her but she could feel the distance between them like a solid barrier. Kind of like the way he'd been after she'd first broken the news that he could be Josh's father and he had switched off that initial interest in *her*.

Was that part of it? The way she'd brushed him off after dinner the other night? Was he backing away from Josh because of *that*? Oh…why on earth had she given in to that temptation to kiss him? Maybe he thought she was playing games. Flirting and then playing hard to get. It might have been misguided but all she'd been trying to do was take the significance out of that first kiss. Put them on friendly terms but nothing more.

But now she seemed to be in exactly the scenario she'd been trying to avoid by not letting herself get too close to Rick. It wasn't supposed to backfire like this.

'Do you want to watch Harry Potter again?'

'No.'

'How 'bout we look at some of the maths Miss Allen sent in?'

'*No-o-o.*' Josh shook his head with miserable jerks. 'I'm too tired. I feel sick.'

Sarah's heart skipped a beat. It was so hard to stop her voice getting instantly tighter and higher. 'What kind of sick?'

'I'm hot. And my back hurts.'

Oh…God. They were living on such a knife-edge now. These few weeks following the transplant were the most critical. It took time for the transplanted bone marrow to migrate into the bone cavities. To engraft and start doing their job of producing normal blood cells. Until then, Josh was at high risk of infection or excessive bleeding. Blood samples were being taken daily to monitor whether engraftment was taking place and to watch organ function. Josh was being given multiple antibiotics along with anti-rejection drugs on top of what had become his normal drug regime. He would also receive blood and platelet transfusions as required.

Mike had warned them that it was normal for a bone-marrow-transplant patient to feel very sick and weak. Josh would experience nausea and vomiting, diarrhoea and extreme weakness. The possible complications he had talked to Sarah about included infection, bleeding, graft versus host disease and liver disease. Mouth ulcers and temporary confusion seemed minor in comparison but could still add a new level of misery.

So many things could go wrong and even the slightest symptom Josh experienced created a wave of panic that was pointless but inevitable. He said he felt hot. Was he running a temperature? Could he have already picked up a bug of some kind? A sore back might indicate a problem with his kidneys. Or maybe his liver. He was pale and tired enough to look as though a blood transfusion might be on the cards. Sarah fought the panic. She even managed to keep her voice sounding perfectly calm.

'I'll get Katie to call Doctor Mike and he can come and have a look at you.'

Josh nodded. He lay on his bed and stared at the ceiling.

'Shall I take today's picture for the cork board?'

He shook his head.

'We could put a different picture up. Do you want to choose one from the ones I cut out of the house magazines? The kind of house we might want to live in one day?' Sarah was feeling desperate. 'The one with the garden for the dog, remember?'

Josh sighed. His lip quivered. 'I like Rick's house,' he said in a small voice.

'It hasn't got a garden.' Sarah kicked herself mentally for the negative comment and searched wildly for a way to repair the unhappy silence that fell. 'There's lots of houses that would be close to Rick's house though. In Port Chalmers.'

Would she want to live that far away from work? Practically on Rick's doorstep? Yes…if it made Josh happy.

'That might be OK.' He seemed to be thinking

about it but then he pushed at his bed cover. 'I want to go to the toilet.'

Sarah nodded. 'Come on, then.' She stood on the pedal at the end of the bed to lower it as far as it could go. Then she drew the covers back to free his legs. She put her arm around Josh to support him as he began to stand up but he pulled away irritably.

'I don't need help.'

'OK.'

This was the hardest part. The way Josh was so determined to be independent when it was obviously getting to be more of a struggle every day. He'd lost so much weight in the last week and his strength was not up to making his body move the way he wanted it to. Sarah could only hover by his side as he hung on to his IV stand, pushing it slowly ahead of him to get to the bathroom. He hated using a bedpan or bottle so much that if he ever agreed to it, Sarah would know he was dangerously ill. So it was good that he was still insisting on taking these steps to look after things himself.

'Don't come in.'

'Only if you leave the door open just a little bit.'

He conceded half an inch of a gap. Thank goodness the door didn't have any kind of lock. Sarah hated being even this far away where she wouldn't be able to catch him if he fell. He let Katie go in with him but no one else. Sarah rested her forehead against the wall and took in a slow breath.

Rick might have been allowed to accompany him.

Josh needed him here. Nobody could say how much of an effect someone's psychological well-being had on their physical condition but it was obvious that the happier someone was, the better they could heal. And even if it didn't have a measurable effect on the kinds of things they could monitor with all this high-tech equipment, it would make these weeks that much more bearable. For everyone.

She had to talk to Rick about this, but how? She couldn't do it in the room with Josh because

ALISON ROBERTS   197

it was quite likely that the conversation would have to include being open about the attraction between them. If he was asleep it might be OK but the last time Rick had come through the door and seen Josh asleep he'd said he'd come back later and he'd slipped out again too fast for Sarah to say anything. Non-verbal communication even to indicate the need to talk to him was going to be difficult as well, given the way his gaze seemed to slide away the instant it caught hers.

Sarah heard the sound of the toilet being flushed and breathed a sigh of relief. In a short time she would have Josh safely back in his bed where she could watch over him.

With the relief came a new thought. Would it make a difference if she was honest about finding Rick attractive? That she was being pulled so close, so fast that she knew she could fall in love with him far, far too easily?

But then what? She'd feel like she was selling herself for Josh's sake. Forcing Rick into playing the role of being a father. Never knowing if he was around because of Josh or because of her.

What if Josh somehow sensed that Rick's interest had to do with more than being a dad?

Back to square one. He would be devastated.

She couldn't win. What was best for Josh, what *she* wanted, what was possibly going through Rick's head, was filling her own mind. Endlessly going round and round. Confusing her. Ramping up a tension that was quite bad enough all on its own.

The dog was the last straw.

Sitting there, outside the gourmet hamburger shop, with its big, sad eyes fixed on Rick while he waited for his order to be filled.

It reminded him of the look on Sarah's face when he'd gone to visit Josh on his way home. The gazes had held a plea he couldn't respond to. Wanted something from him that he wasn't capable of delivering even if he'd *wanted* to. Which he didn't.

Dammit. As if today hadn't been hard enough already.

That session, with Simon's mother sitting in

his office in floods of tears. Simon's coma had lightened a little and the boy was responsive to painful stimuli but he hadn't opened his eyes in nearly two weeks. Hadn't responded to his mother's voice or squeezed his dad's hand or given any hope that he might come back as more than a physical shell of the child they'd known and loved.

It was early days yet, Rick had reassured the mother. Simon was young and healthy. His EEG showed a good amount of brain activity. It was too soon to give up hope.

But fear and exhaustion had taken a huge toll. Simon's mother was facing the possibility of having a severely brain-damaged son.

'I should have made the most of every moment,' she'd sobbed. 'Why did I waste those moments by telling him off about how messy his room was or sending him outside to scrape the mud off his rugby boots? Why didn't we take him to Disneyland years ago instead of worrying about how fast we could pay off the mortgage? What if...?' She'd stopped, staring at Rick in utter desolation. 'What if I never hear him say "I love you, Mum" again?'

The words had haunted Rick all day.

What if there came a time when Rick knew he'd never see that smart, funny, brave kid who happened to be *his* son again? If he found himself having an agonised conversation with Max or Jet and saying *he* should have made the most of every moment?

But how could he when he was so aware of Sarah every time he even walked into the bone-marrow unit? Knowing that she would be there in the room? That he would have to keep his guard up and make sure he didn't give out any signals about the effect she had on him? Knowing that if he did, she'd just brush him off as unimportant. No big deal. He wasn't worth a position of anything more than Josh's father because he'd treated her sister so badly he'd made sure that she would never realise her dream of a complete family.

Well, that was fine. He didn't want it to be a big deal. Having a sick kid was enough of a complication in his life. He just didn't want the aggravation of having to be so close to the untouchable Sarah adding its own tension.

'Here you go, mate. Lamb burger and kumera wedges. Extra mint yoghurt on the side.'

'Cheers.' Rick managed a smile. 'Now I'll just have to get past the potential ambush at the door.'

The man serving him looked over his shoulder and groaned. 'That mutt back again? I'll have to ring the council in the morning. I called them last week and they're obviously not doing their job properly. Typical! Why do we bother paying our rates, huh?'

No doubt he'd give the council an earful tomorrow. They'd make an extra effort to find the dog and lock him into a cage. They'd wait the required length of time for someone to claim it, was it ten days? And then, if nobody came, they'd dispose of it. End of story.

An old bell clanged as Rick pushed open the door and stepped into the street. He couldn't help glancing down at the dog.

At least Josh would never know what its fate had been.

The dog grinned up at him, flattening its ears and waving its tail.

'Oh, for God's sake…' Rick opened the bag he was holding and fished a piece of the lamb steak out of the burger. He threw it and the dog caught the food with a flash of white teeth. It practically inhaled it.

Rick walked on. It wasn't far to the warehouse and he'd felt the need to stretch his legs so he hadn't bothered to bring a vehicle. Half a block later, he realised he wasn't alone.

'Go home,' he told the dog sternly. 'You must have one.'

It had been stupid to give it any food. The dog clearly thought he could solve all its problems now. It was staying a respectful distance behind him but it was still there as he turned up his driveway.

'Look, I'll give you some more food,' he said. 'And then you can go home. OK?'

He wasn't going to sacrifice the rest of his

dinner but he emptied half the bag of kumera wedges onto the side of the driveway and then resolutely went inside and closed his door. The dog would be gone by morning. At least it wouldn't still be miserably hungry when the dog catcher found it and it wasn't as if he could do any more to help the mutt.

So why did he feel that, despite doing his best, he was still somehow failing everyone?

The dog.

Simon.

Sarah.

Josh.

Himself…?

Life never used to be this complicated. If this was what finally growing up was all about, maybe he'd had the right idea in postponing it for so long.

She was waiting for him this time.

This was the fourth time Sarah had slipped out of Josh's room to hover in the unit's reception area. The desk was only staffed during working hours so it had been deserted for quite some time now. The nursing staff were either busy with patients or in the central office further down the corridor. If any of them knew where she was, they would assume she needed a bit of peace and quiet and room to stretch her legs just a little after the strain of a long and difficult day.

Josh had developed pain that needed more medication but that had made him vomit and he'd needed yet more drugs to control the nausea. There'd been a blood transfusion this afternoon and along with new pain and the monitoring and extra tests, Josh hadn't had a chance to rest properly. He'd been awake and fretful and asking, at regular intervals, when his dad was going to come and visit.

And now it was 7:00 p.m. and Rick still hadn't showed his face. If he didn't appear in the next few minutes, Sarah was going to call him at home and give him a piece of her mind about letting a sick little boy down. She was furious. Pacing back and forth across the reception area wasn't helping at all. Seeing Rick finally come through the double doors that led to the main hospital didn't help either. If anything, it bent and broke the last of her self-control.

'Where have you *been* all day, Rick? Josh has been asking and asking for you.'

'I'm here now.' He sounded weary. As though he was only here because it was something he was required to do. An extra duty to tick off for the working day.

'He's asleep,' Sarah informed him icily. 'Probably for the night.'

'Oh...' Rick's gaze slid away. 'I'll come back in the morning, then.'

'Sure...' Sarah watched him turn away. She harnessed her anger and let it escape in a sarcastic tone. 'If it's convenient, of course.'

He turned back. He pushed stiff fingers through his hair. 'I've had a busy day,' he said quietly. 'I've got a thirteen-year-old boy in Intensive Care who's in trouble. He started having seizures and—'

'You've got a nine-year-old *son* who's in trouble,' Sarah snapped. 'And you haven't been any-where near him.'

Rick sighed. 'I'm here now.'

'Too little,' Sarah snarled. 'And too late. He's had a horrible day and the one thing that could have made it better might have been having a visit from his dad, and it didn't happen. What's going on here, Rick? You've been avoiding him for days. Has the novelty worn off or something?'

Rick gave an incredulous huff. 'I've been in to see him every single day.'

'Only once. You used to come two or three times, remember? Set a precedent with kids and they have this funny trust that it's going to carry on. They're a bit like dogs that way.'

He seemed to wince at the comparison. He opened his mouth to say something but Sarah didn't give him the chance.

'You said you'd give being a dad your best shot.' Sarah tried to sound accusing but the tell-tale wobble in her voice was a sure sign tears weren't far away. She needed to wrap this up fast. 'If this is your best shot, it's not good enough.

It would have been better not to get involved with Josh at all than to let him think you cared and then—' she had to swallow to get rid of the sudden lump in her throat '—avoid him like this. It's not fair, Rick...' Her voice had lost all its power now. It was hardly more than a whisper. 'It's not even nice.'

'I'm not avoiding Josh.'

'You *are*.' For once, Sarah managed to catch and hold Rick's gaze. 'You might not think so but that's what it's like on this side of the equation. You hardly come and when you do you don't stay very long. You're avoiding him.'

'I'm not.'

It felt like Rick's gaze was holding hers now, instead of the other way round. His features softened. His eyes were dark and intense but one corner of his mouth lifted in a wry, lopsided smile.

'I'm not avoiding Josh,' Rick said. 'I'm avoiding *you*.'

'Why? What have I done?'

'It's more what I've done. Or maybe what I want to do.'

Sarah swallowed hard. Here it was, out in the open. They had the chance to talk about this and get it sorted. For Josh's sake. She took a quick breath as she screwed up her courage.

'Tell me,' she whispered.

But Rick jerked his head in a sharp, negative gesture and made a rough sound that could have been a strangled groan. He was about to turn away but Sarah grabbed his arm and tugged so that he had to face her again and somehow it had brought them even closer together.

'Rick...*please*... We have to talk about this. I need to understand.'

The movement of his throat suggested he was finding it difficult to swallow. When he spoke, she hardly recognised the deep drawl.

'*This* is what I'm talking about...'

She knew what was coming the moment Rick began to pull her into his arms. She also knew that this was going be nothing like the brief, almost impersonal kisses they'd already given each other. He was moving in for the real thing.

She could have pulled free. She knew quite well that if she'd made any protest, Rick would have let her go instantly, but if he did, he'd probably walk out and they would never have the chance to talk. She'd be left still angry and confused and miserable and would have to stay that way...maybe for ever.

She might spend the rest of her life wondering what it would have been like to be properly kissed by Rick Wilson.

And...she deserved just a moment for herself, didn't she? Time out from being mother to a suffering child. A respite from remembering all the misery of today's procedures and problems and imagining what was still to come. A bit of nostalgia, even, for a time when she had had no one to be responsible for other than herself and men had made her feel desirable.

Was it so wrong to want to feel wanted?

Even if it was, she was powerless to resist the pull. The pull into Rick's arms and into the delicious heat of desire. Tiny flames that ignited at the mere touch of his hands and exploded into a blinding white heat as his mouth shaped itself to cover hers.

No chance of pulling free now. The possibility didn't even occur to Sarah as she closed her eyes and lifted her arms to wrap them around Rick's neck.

No. There was no way out of this.

She was completely lost.

CHAPTER EIGHT

THIS was the most astonishing kiss of his life.

The feel of Sarah's mouth under his. So soft, so sweet, so…responsive. The way her whole body seemed to soften in his arms so that merely the desire to mould her closer to his own body seemed to be enough to make it happen.

He'd known it would be this perfect that first moment he'd set eyes on her. What he hadn't realised was that it would feel so…*right*.

He could let his hands roam and shape her breasts. Or cup her bottom and pull her against the urgent need pulsing in his core. He could peel away her clothing and then his own and he *knew* there would be none of that first-time awkwardness. They would just morph from a first kiss into being lovers and it would be like they'd always been together, only better. Much better, because it would still have all the excitement of being totally new.

Of course, he couldn't do any of that. Not here. He might be so involved in this kiss that he wouldn't care if half of Queen Mary's medical staff had gathered to watch in this reception area but he wasn't insane. Some things... OK, a great many things that he intended to do to Sarah Prescott needed complete privacy.

For a moment he let himself revel in the anticipation of those things but when it threatened to become too powerful to resist, he eased himself away from her. Reluctantly. Just his lips to start with.

'Come with me,' he murmured. 'I know a much better place for this.'

He felt the way her body tensed. It was slow process, like the development of one of those Polaroid pictures he took for Josh. Was she having that much trouble focusing because of that kiss? He liked that idea. Enough to make him close that tiny distance between them. He wanted to scramble her brain all over again and make her aware of only him and what he could do to her senses.

But Sarah resisted this time. Her hands slid over his shoulders to rest on his chest. She even pushed at him faintly. And she shook her head. She seemed ready to say something but no words emerged from her parted lips. Rick could sense a growing distress. Capturing her hand, he led her to one of the armchairs. He needed to reassure her somehow. Good grief, this wasn't *that* big a deal. He was talking about sex here. Potentially mind-blowingly good sex. But it wasn't as if he was planning to disrupt her entire life. Or his, of course.

Sarah's legs buckled without hesitation and she sat down. He perched on the edge of the adjacent chair, still keeping her hand firmly clasped in his.

He raised an eyebrow as he smiled gently. 'Problem?'

Sarah shook her head but then she nodded. 'I can't...*we* can't...'

'Why not?' It seemed such a no-brainer to him

now that he knew she was as interested as he was. They'd be seeing quite a lot of each other from now on so why not make it a whole heap more enjoyable?

The tiny huff of breath from Sarah told him that the answer should be obvious.

'Because of Josh.'

Rick considered that. He might have expected her to say *because of Lucy*. Or because she knew he was a rat or because she wasn't really interested. No, he knew that one wasn't true. He had to hide the way his lips wanted to curl again. Nobody could kiss like that if they weren't interested. Very, very interested.

'This is about us, Sarah,' he said slowly. 'It has nothing to do with Josh.'

'How can you say that? You're his father.'

'True.' Amazing how he didn't have the slightest hesitation in agreeing to that statement now. He couldn't imagine denying it, in fact.

'You're going to be part of his life, for a long time. I hope,' she added after the tiniest hesitation.

This wasn't the time to be talking about prognoses. 'I will,' Rick said confidently.

A faint warning bell was sounding somewhere in the back of his mind. Heralding concern about that 'part of his life'. That more could well be expected of him than he felt willing or capable of giving.

'And I'm a part of his life, too. It's all connected.'

The bell got louder. Connections. Expectations... Rick could almost feel a mental door closing, shutting off the sound. Listening instead to the husky note in Sarah's voice that advertised her arousal. This was about now. About *them*. The strength of his desire for what the next hour or two could hold was more than enough to make any further thought into the future irrelevant.

He nodded, more an acceptance of the direction of his own thoughts than anything Sarah had just said. He had loosened his hold on her hand now and was stroking her palm with his thumb. Feeling the shape of all the tiny bones in there. When he moved his fingers as well, he could feel the way her fingers and knuckles moved. Whether she was aware of it or not, her hand was responding to his touch. A discreet, intimate little dance.

'And that's a bad thing?' he queried softly.

He heard another small huff. Or maybe it was a sigh at his lack of comprehension.

'My relationship with Josh is one thing,' he said. 'My relationship with you is something else. We could be—'

'Friends,' Sarah interrupted. That huskiness in her voice had increased. She sounded almost hoarse now. 'Friends would be good.'

'Absolutely.' Rick closed his hand around hers to increase the pressure of his touch. 'Good friends.' He waited until she looked up. '*Very* good friends.'

He smiled at her with the most winning expression he could muster. It wasn't a hard call. He had a lot to lose.

Sarah's hair rippled with the subtle shake she gave her head. It was enough to catch the light over the reception desk and send a shower of golden sparks over her head. 'And if it didn't work? If we stopped being such good *friends*?' There was another play of light through her hair. 'It would be Josh who'd catch the fallout, Rick. I can't let that happen. You're important to him. I don't think you have any idea how important you've already become to Josh.'

Rick stifled the urge to catch a handful of her hair and move it so he could see more of those glints. She was worried that whatever was happening between them was going to fizzle out in no time flat. Maybe she thought all he wanted was a one-night stand like he'd had with her sister.

It wasn't true. This was a very different proposition. *He* was a very different person. He didn't want a one-night stand. Good grief, no. He wanted…he wanted…

The answer wasn't there but it didn't matter because Rick at least knew what he didn't want and that was to lose the opportunity to get to know Sarah a lot better. To just *be* with her. The future would take care of itself. It always had, hadn't it?

'Josh is important to me, too,' he said sincerely. 'So are you, Sarah. I'm attracted to you.' He grinned. 'Just in case that wasn't already clear.'

Sarah ducked her head with an endearingly shy movement. 'It was,' she murmured.

Rick grinned. 'Well, you did say you needed to understand what was bothering me.'

He let his breath out in a sigh. 'I want to be with you,' he continued in a much more serious tone. 'So much that it *has* been interfering with how often I've been coming to see Josh. I'm sorry about that. I was trying to avoid torturing myself and it was selfish and…immature.' He tried to smile again but it was a crooked effort. 'I am trying to grow up. Honest.'

The huff was laughter this time but he could also see a shine in Sarah's eyes that had nothing to do the light over the reception desk so it had to be from tears.

'I'm sorry I ever said that you needed to grow up, Rick. You're perfect just the way you are.'

The words gave him a very odd sensation inside. As though something was melting. No... more like expanding. A bubble of something shiny that would pop and send a glow right through him. She thought he was perfect? Oh... *man*...

He had to concentrate on finding the right words. 'Josh is my son,' he managed. 'And I'll start being better at letting him know how important that is. Nothing's going to change that, including whatever might happen between us... if we let it.'

'But...' He watched the way Sarah caught her bottom lip between her teeth and felt a stab of renewed desire deep in his belly. 'What if it's just...physical?'

Rick raised an eyebrow. 'Are you going to avoid any kind of relationship because you've become Josh's mum?'

'I...um...haven't given it any thought. It's...' Sarah sighed heavily, clearly releasing something she hadn't intended to admit. 'OK, I haven't met anyone who's made me think about it. The fact that you're Josh's dad makes it...complicated.'

'But mightn't it be even more complicated with someone who wasn't Josh's dad? Given what happened in your last relationship?'

That seemed to score a point, judging by the way Sarah frowned at the reminder.

'I don't—'

'Sarah...' Rick put both his hands over hers. 'If you think about worst-case scenarios you'd never do anything in life. And if you live in the past or in the future, you risk missing what's happening in the present and that's...well, that's your life.'

She didn't say anything but her gaze was locked on his. She was certainly listening.

'We're in the present. The person I used to be—that Lucy met—is long gone. This is now. My attraction to you is now and it's real. We're both grown-ups.' He paused just long enough for a quick smile. 'I'm getting there, anyway. None of us know what the future holds. If this thing—whatever it is—between us doesn't go anywhere, we can handle it. Look at all the divorced people out there who manage to co-parent their kids just fine.'

'That's true…I guess.'

'And it's not as if we're planning something heavy like marriage.' Rick did his best to make that sound like the only really big deal there could be. 'Think of it as stress relief if you like. You deserve it.'

Once more, he lowered his tone and slowed his speech so that when the words came out they sounded more solemn than anything he'd ever heard himself utter.

'I promise I won't let it hurt Josh.'

A silence fell. They were still connected by their eye contact and the way their hands were tangled together. He could *feel* her. Body and soul.

'Let's just think about the present,' he said softly. 'You and me. What we want. I know what *I* want.' He paused again, holding her gaze and her hands. Trying to draw her closer to him by sheer willpower. 'What do *you* want?'

'*You.*' The word was a whisper.

Rick leaned close enough to brush her lips with his. 'Come with me, then.'

'I can't go home with you, Rick. It's too far. Today's been—'

'I'm not taking you that far. There's an on-call room that's got my name on it for the night. It's private. It's got a bed.'

She caught her breath in a tiny gasp. He watched the way her pupils dilated, making her eyes dark with desire.

'You might get called.'

'I'm not actually on call. I just didn't want to be too far away in case something goes wrong for Simon again.'

'Simon?'

'The boy in ICU. The one I've been struggling to get stable again today. He's looking good at the moment. Better than he has been, in fact. It's highly unlikely that I'll get called.'

He stood up, still holding her hand, but he didn't pull her to her feet. This had to be her choice.

He saw the way she took a deep breath as she

made that choice. Time stopped for a moment, kind of like the way it had when he'd first seen her. This decision was as important as her arrival in his life. Right now, it felt as if his life depended on it.

Sarah got to her feet. He felt her hold on his hand tighten. Her answer was in the slightly tremulous smile she gave him. Rick didn't feel the need to say anything more either.

Hand in hand, they went through the double doors into the main block.

Sarah was grateful for the strength she could feel in Rick's hand and the way he was gently guiding her.

Her brain felt as confused as it had been for some time now but it was as though a coin had been flipped. Instead of that endless circuit of denial and frustration and worry and guilt, this was a jumble of the promise of ultimate pleasure laced with good reasons for permission to experience it.

She knew there were plenty of flaws in Rick's

point of view. Like the way some children could be used as pawns in the games played by parents whose divorce was less than amicable. And that while it was true her last boyfriend had dumped her because of Josh, he'd been presented with the unexpected addition of a child in the equation well after the relationship had started. It would be different if she met someone now.

Counter-arguments that could have under-mined Rick's persuasive efforts were locked away, however, and if Sarah tried to access that part of her brain, she became aware of a flood of irresistible sensation instead. The way Rick looked at her in the lift. The way he locked the door of the tiny room upstairs and pinned her against it to kiss her. Not on her lips but on the side of her neck, exactly where she could feel her pulse stumbling with unbearable anticipation. The feel of his lips and the touch of his tongue went straight into her bloodstream and coursed through her body, igniting fierce desire in her belly and making her legs weak.

He undressed her with the kind of expertise

that should have reminded her of his past and rung alarm bells, but they'd been silenced along with the counter arguments. Worry about Josh needing her was tucked away as well. She had her mobile phone. The nurses could contact her if she was needed.

Sarah gave herself up to what she wanted most and she wanted to believe everything Rick had said. And it was easy because she recognised the truth of it. Angsting over the past—including Rick's playboy antics and her sister's part in them—or worrying about the future that encompassed how she could deal with the fallout this might produce could totally override what was happening right now and *this* was the moment she was living.

As herself. Not as an aunt or mother or sister. Or a guardian or nurse.

This was about what was at the centre of her being. What she loved and wanted. And it tapped into long-neglected hopes and dreams. It was...

Heaven.

Rick's hands and lips roamed her body and

brought so many nerve endings to life her skin was on fire. Her own hands and lips were further conduits of the incredible heat as they made contact with Rick's skin. The firmness of his chest, the silky skin interrupted by whorls of soft hair. The softness of his lips and the delicious scrape of a rough jaw. The fresh taste of his mouth and the heady musk of far more intimate parts of his body.

This was urgent, this first time. Pent-up desire claimed precedence and Sarah heard herself begging for Rick to take her. She wanted him inside her. She wanted to wrap her legs and arms around him and hang on for dear life as they rode this unbelievable wave of sensation.

They were both gasping for breath by the time reality had a chance to intrude. A tangle of limbs in a bed that should have been too narrow for what they had just accomplished. This was the moment when things could have become awkward. When any doubts in her head were released to roam free and potential complications could bring a vanguard of regret.

Sarah was afraid to open her mouth in case words were the key so she stayed silent, trying to hold on to the astonishing feeling of being exactly where she was supposed to be. The place she'd been searching for her whole life without realising it. Rick was also silent.

Verbally, anyway. His hands were speaking for him. Touching her body with what felt like reverence. Smoothing long strands of her tumbled hair from where it had stuck to perspiration-dampened skin on her breasts and face.

And then he kissed her lips. Slowly. With a tenderness that washed away the possibility of allowing any doubts significant head space. She couldn't let this go. It was worth keeping, no matter what. It was worth fighting for with everything she had.

'Next time,' Rick murmured against her lips, 'we'll go slow. OK?'

Sarah simply smiled. He felt it and let his breath out in a satisfied sigh.

Next time wouldn't be tonight. They both knew that. This uninterrupted privacy had been a gift. Too precious to risk by taking advantage of it. But Rick seemed as happy as Sarah was to linger just a little longer. She was loving the latent strength she could feel in the arms holding her so gently. She wanted to soak in the rise and fall of his chest against hers. The strong, steady beat of his heart and the soft tickle of his breath on her face.

She would remember all these things with such clarity. She would be able to pull them around her like the softest blanket when she needed comfort as she went to sleep alone in the corner of Josh's room.

The need to be back there returned so gradually it seemed a mutual agreement when they untangled themselves and got dressed again. The process was interrupted more than once as they brushed against each other in the small space and had to pause and touch properly. To hold and kiss each other.

But finally they were back at the double doors leading to the bone-marrow unit.

'Shall I come in? In case Josh wakes up?'

'I'll tell him you'll be coming tomorrow. In the morning?'

'First thing,' Rick promised. 'I'm going to go and check on Simon now and then I might go home for a bit. There's something I should check on. It might need feeding.'

Sarah blinked up at him. 'Feeding? It's alive?'

'If it hasn't been caught.' Rick was smiling. 'That dog Josh saw that day? It followed me home last night and it was still sitting in my driveway this morning.'

'Oh…' Josh would be *so* happy to hear that. So excited. He would be pulled into his dream of a perfect future. Transported.

Kind of like the way she'd felt in Rick's arms such a short time ago?

'Should I tell him, do you think?'

Rick understood instantly. The concern that darkened his eyes to ink showed how fast his thoughts meshed with hers. He knew how much it would mean to Josh. What the repercussions might be further down the track.

'Leave it with me,' he said. 'I might have an idea.'

With another soft kiss, he was gone. Sarah was left watching the space he had vanished into beyond the doors.

She wrapped her arms around herself. He had understood. He cared enough to take a share of the burden with the intention of making it lighter somehow.

For her? For Josh?

It didn't matter. She loved him for it.

Or maybe she'd already been loving him and the combination of tonight's revelations had simply allowed her to recognise the truth of it.

There was no going back. It was frightening but it was wonderful and it was happening now.

'One day at a time,' she whispered. Only now the mantra held the promise of a dream. Something to hang on to, not endure.

CHAPTER NINE

THIS day just kept getting better and better.

Rick had had a very early start. He'd been dreaming about Sarah and he was still thinking about her as he watched the sun come up over the harbour and bring the world back to life. He didn't bother with breakfast because he had too much to do but when he finally got close to arriving at work, he stopped in at a fast-food restaurant and bought bacon-and-egg muffins and French fries. A supremely unhealthy meal but Josh seemed to be through the bad spell of the last couple of days and it might tempt him to eat something.

It did. He took several bites of the muffin and slowly nibbled his way through half the little paper bag of salty fries. Sarah looked so happy it was hard not to grin like an idiot every time he looked at her.

Which he found himself doing at rather frequent intervals. Ever since the dramatic change in their relationship the night before last, the atmosphere in Josh's room had been like being on a different planet. So much of the tension was gone it had become a happy place. Positive. Filled with an intense anticipation of good things to come. Not that he and Sarah had made it back to the on-call room or anywhere else that private but they knew they would. Soon.

They'd managed a quick coffee together a couple of times and lunch in the cafeteria yesterday, which had been great because when he was away from Josh's room Rick didn't have to be careful of how often he looked at her. He could even touch her discreetly. Fingertip to fingertip as their hands lay on the table. A hand on her back that could slide down to that delicious curve of her rump as he ushered her through a doorway. A stolen kiss between floors on an elevator.

By tacit consent, they were keeping this new development secret because this was between them and neither wanted it to impinge on their relationships with Josh. The reminder of the small boy who had brought them together but was making this new relationship more complicated was always there. Conversations always included him. How he was feeling. What the latest results of tests might mean. What plans they could come up with that might entertain him.

'What happened about the dog?' Sarah had asked at lunch yesterday. 'Was he still there in your driveway?'

Rick had shaken his head sadly. 'No sign of it. Sorry.'

He'd seen the sparkle in her eyes fade to disappointment but he hadn't said anything else. Today he would. Later. He had some work to do first and even that was adding to the satisfaction of this particular day.

Up in the ICU, Simon was showing a dramatic improvement in his condition.

'He opened his eyes,' his mother told Rick. 'He squeezed my hand and—'

'And he said "Mum",' his father added, when his wife was too overcome to continue. 'He recognised her and he can *talk*. He's coming out of his coma, isn't he, Doc?'

'Sure looks like it.' Rick was only too happy to share the joy. He spent longer than necessary checking his young patient. Simon was deeply asleep again but this was a turning point. It wasn't going to be easy or quick but they all had reason for genuine hope now that he might recover.

Rick floated through the rest of his rounds and an outpatient clinic, knowing that the best of this day was still to come. Late that afternoon, he went back to Josh's room. His son's eyes widened when he saw what Rick had brought into the room with him.

'What's that for?'

'You.' Rick gave the wheelchair a bit of a twirl. 'Thought you might like to see something other than these four walls.'

Sarah looked horrified. 'He can't go out of here.'

'He's allowed to,' Rick assured her. 'He'll have to wear a gown and mask and some gloves and we won't go anywhere there's a lot of people. He's been in strict isolation for a while now and something a bit more exciting could be very good. That is, if he feels up to a wee adventure.' He turned back to Josh. 'How 'bout it, buddy?'

Josh was already starting to climb out of his bed. 'Where are we going?'

'It's a surprise.'

Sarah was looking almost as undecided as the moment before Rick had persuaded her to go to bed with him. He smiled at her, holding her gaze, sending her a message he hoped she would read and accept.

Trust me.

She didn't smile back but she did release the breath she'd been holding and nod faintly. She helped Josh into the wheelchair and found the protective clothing he would need. Rick carefully transferred the bag of IV fluid to the pole attached to the side of the basket on the back of the wheelchair. He also picked up the Polaroid camera and put it into the basket.

He took them out of the bone-marrow unit, along the corridor and into an elevator that was only for staff use. On the basement floor he propelled the chair along deserted corridors past places like the medical records department and a prosthetic limb workshop.

'Where are we going?' Josh piped insistently more than once.

'There's something I want you to see,' was all Rick said.

There was an isolated parking area down here that gave access to delivery trucks and vehicles that needed to arrive discreetly. Rick was keeping his fingers crossed that a hearse wasn't due to make a collection. There were windows that looked out onto the bare concrete at the bottom of a ramp that led to ground level. There was a vehicle there but it was the one Rick was expecting. A grunty four-wheel drive. Max was in the driver's seat and gave him a thumbs-up before jumping out and going round to the back.

'What on earth…?' Sarah murmured.

Max opened the back door of his vehicle and a large shape emerged.

'Oh…' Josh tried to stand up in the wheel-chair and Rick had to steady him with a hand on one of his shoulders. The frailty of the bones he could feel made something twist, deep inside. So did the way Josh's scalp showed more and more through the little that remained of his hair.

'You said he wasn't there any more!' Sarah exclaimed.

'He wasn't. The dog catcher had taken him to the pound.'

Josh managed to drag his eyes away from the window and look up at Rick. Sarah was staring at him, too.

'The council knew him well. There'd been complaints about him for weeks, ever since he'd escaped from the pound when they first caught him. Nobody had claimed him then. He's not registered or microchipped or anything and they were only too happy to let him go to a good home.'

'But…' There was a flash of alarm in Sarah's face. 'How are you going to keep a dog at your place?'

'I'm not. That's where Max and Ellie come in. They're happy to look after him for the moment.' Rick was trying to give Sarah a very reassuring look. He had taken care of every possibility here. But she still looked worried. As if he was presenting her with a major problem of having to find somewhere new to live the moment Josh was released from hospital.

'Max and Ellie think he's wonderful,' he added quietly. 'If things don't pan out, they're more than happy to adopt him permanently. Josh could visit any time he wanted.'

'*No.*' Josh was staring fiercely out of the window again. Max had come closer and they were only a short distance on the other side of the glass. The dog was sitting, staring back at Josh, his ears flattened and his tail waving madly. 'He's *my* dog.'

A heartbeat of eye contact between Rick and Sarah said it all. This kind of joy could speed his recovery. And if the worst happened and Josh didn't make it through this, the dog wasn't simply being used and discarded. He had a back-up family. Sarah's smile wobbled and Rick had to look away.

'He hasn't got a name yet.' Rick crouched beside the wheelchair, focusing on Josh to give Sarah a moment. 'Max and I thought you should do the honours.'

Josh had a dreamy look on his face now. 'Can I go outside and pat him?'

'Not today, mate. Sorry.' Rick was busy with the camera now. He took a photo that got Josh and the dog locked in joyous communion through the sheet of glass. 'He can come and visit again when you've got a few good blood cells ready to fight off bugs.'

'I'm getting better,' Josh said, still fierce. 'It won't be long, will it?'

'No.' Sarah sounded like she was still trying

not to cry. She cleared her throat. 'He looks cleaner than he did last time we saw him.'

'He's had a bath. Been de-wormed and de-fleaed. He's a new dog.'

'He's really hairy.'

'That's what I'm going to call him,' Josh said.

'What? Hairy?'

'No. Harry. Like Harry Potter.'

'Hairy Harry.' Rick grinned. 'Cool.'

Max waved apologetically. A laundry truck was at the top of the ramp. He walked back to his car and pointed to the rear hatch. Harry obediently leapt inside.

'He's really smart, isn't he?' Josh said happily.

'Sure is. Time for him to go home, though, and time for you to get back to bed. It's almost your dinnertime.'

But Josh was way too excited to want to eat. He was clutching the photograph and grinning from ear to ear. Sarah eyed the tray of food and looked worried.

'Tell you what.' Rick was brimming over with inspiration today. 'I'll stay with Josh and read him a story or talk dogs or something. He'll settle down and I'll get his dinner reheated. Why don't you go and pamper yourself for an hour or two?'

'What?'

'Must be a while since you've got out of here properly.' Rick let his gaze remind her of the most recent, memorable break she'd had and he enjoyed watching the colour rise in her cheeks. 'You could go shopping maybe?'

'I could pop back to the apartment, I guess. I could do with some different clothes and a soak in a bath.'

'Mmm. Sounds…nice.' Rick's drawl was only intended to sound encouraging but it obviously occurred to both of them at the same time that sharing a bath needed to go on the list of future activities.

Sarah's colour went up a notch. 'Well…if it's OK with Josh.'

'It's cool.' Josh sounded offhand. He didn't look up from the photo. 'See you later. And can you bring a new battery for my Gameboy?'

'Sure.'

With Sarah gone, Rick settled down to talk dogs and whatever else took Josh's fancy. He was happy. More than happy. Today had gone even better than he'd planned. This being a part-time dad thing wasn't so bad. In fact, how lucky was he? How many guys could get presented with such a great kid who was so easy to make happy? And how many would get the incredible bonus thrown in of a gorgeous woman who also seemed very easy to make happy?

Josh went from being wide awake and excited to sound asleep within the first pages of the story he'd chosen but Rick was more than content to stay in the armchair and contemplate how good he was feeling. And how much better he would be when he got the chance to make Sarah very happy again.

Maybe later tonight? He might just make an enquiry as to whether there was a free on-call room. It wasn't as if they had to worry about getting a babysitter at the last minute. Things might be more complicated once Josh was home again but they'd manage. Of course, it would be nice to whisk Sarah away for a weekend some time but that wasn't really a goer. They'd have to take Josh with them, which wouldn't be so bad, but how could they continue where they'd left off with a kid in the next room? That was way too far out of his realm of experience to seem acceptable.

A sense of urgency sneaked up on him. How much longer would Josh be in here, all going well? Two or three weeks? He released his breath in a sigh. It was a bridge that didn't need crossing yet. He would just have to make the most of every opportunity he had until then.

The apartment had a musty, damp, unused feel to it.

Sarah opened a window or two while she put a load of washing on and sifted through accumulated mail, most of which appeared to be bills. She started a bath running and went to her bedroom to find some fresh clothes to take back to the hospital. Dumping them onto her bed, she went and tipped the remnants of a jar of bath salts into the steaming water and then started to take her clothes off.

Oh…Lord. Why did this simple action take her straight back to when Rick had been doing it for her? The caress of warm, fragrant water as she sank into the bath was equally sensuous. Sarah gave up fighting it and allowed her mind to float in the same kind of pleasurable space her limbs were currently experiencing. She hadn't felt this good in… Heavens…she'd *never* felt this good. Josh was doing well and there was real hope for the future. And there was Rick… The possibilities of what that future might hold had expanded exponentially.

Did he feel anything like as strongly about her as she did about him? Would he fall in love with her? Imagine if he did…if they ended up being a family. A healthy Josh with maybe some younger siblings. With them all living in a house with a garden for Harry to roam in.

That would be…perfect.

By the time Sarah climbed out of the bath she was totally relaxed and buzzing with the joy her fantasies had lured her into. She dried herself, found the prettiest underwear she possessed and then went to pull on the clean jeans from the pile on the bed. She paused with one leg inside them. When had Rick seen her wearing anything other than jeans? That long dress at the wedding didn't count because that was ancient history now. Before she could even have imagined feeling so…happy.

She went back to her wardrobe and searched. She found an old knit dress. Long-sleeved, with a deep scoop neckline. It clung to her body until the hips where it flared into soft folds that swirled around her knees when she did a twirl. It was just right. Nothing over the top but it was different and the deep colour made her eyes an astonishing blue.

Instead of pulling her hair back into the loose braid she usually favoured to keep it under control, Sarah brushed it until it was a sleek, golden river. She made two tiny braids at the front and fastened them at the nape of her neck with a small, diamanté clip. Feeling a little silly, she even put some make-up on.

'Anyone would think you were getting ready for a hot date,' she admonished her reflection. The secret little smile came from nowhere.

Maybe she was.

The effect of the dress was certainly gratifying. Rick's eyes popped when she arrived back at the hospital and stood by the window, waiting a moment before putting on her gown and mask. Josh was propped up on his pillows, picking at a plate of food. He also stared at Sarah.

'You looked really pretty,' he said generously, when she went into the room. He eyed Rick. 'Didn't she?'

'Yeah…' Rick's voice had a gravelly edge that Sarah could feel deep in her belly, like the sparks from the scrape of a match.

'Did you remember the battery?'

'Oh, no! Sorry, Josh, I completely forgot about that. I wonder if the hospital shop is still open?'

Rick checked his watch. 'It's seven-thirty but

they do stay open for evening visiting hours. I could go and have a look.'

Katie came into the room. 'You finished that dinner yet?' she asked Josh. She looked at the plate. 'Hmm. At least you've had something. Anyone else hungry?'

'Starving.' Rick and Sarah spoke at the same time. They looked at each other and smiled.

Josh was watching them. 'You could take Sarah somewhere,' he suggested to Rick. ''Cos she's all dressed up.'

Rick's gaze slid away from Sarah instantly. He shrugged. 'You think?'

Josh nodded.

'But I've already been gone for ages,' Sarah said. 'Don't you want some company?'

'I was asleep while you were gone so I didn't notice.' Josh smiled winningly at his nurse. 'You could keep me company, couldn't you, Katie?'

His smile had been so similar to one of Rick's that Sarah's heart gave an odd little lurch. Would he grow up to be like his dad? She'd love to watch that happen.

'Sure,' Katie said with a grin. 'Go on, you two. Go and have some dinner and let me have some time with my boyfriend here.'

Rick was still being careful not to catch Sarah's gaze and give anything away but her heart was thumping erratically. Josh *wanted* her to date Rick?

That fantasy future she'd conjured up in the bath lost some of its fuzzy edges to take on a more believable shape.

'No worries,' Rick said to Josh. 'We'll see if we can find you a battery along the way.'

'See you later, then, short stuff,' Sarah hoped he couldn't hear the tiny tremor in her voice. 'If you're still awake, that is.'

Josh *was* awake when they finally returned.

Katie gave them an unmistakably knowing smile as she excused herself but Josh seemed too sleepy to notice anything that might have given them away, like Sarah's dress being somewhat crumpled and her eyes glowing like stars. Her hair could do with a brush, too. Rick's fingers itched to bury themselves in its soft length and comb it into less of a tumble.

He was feeling a bit rumpled himself. Maybe next time they should make the effort to hang their clothes up instead of leaving them in a pile on the floor of the on-call room where they'd got trampled in their haste to get horizontal.

Worth it, though. Way better than the first time. Slow and sweet and so good, they'd both forgotten they were hungry for food. The less-than-adequate dinner of sandwiches from a vending machine on the way back downstairs had also been worth it.

Rick was standing close to Sarah. Close enough to be aware of her warmth and the scent he could quite easily become addicted to. She'd said he didn't need to come in and say goodnight to Josh because he'd probably be sound asleep but Rick said he wanted to rescue that photo and put it on the corkboard. If Josh slept with it clutched in his hand, it might get wrecked and it could be a while before he could arrange to get another one.

Josh blinked sleepily at them. He'd obviously

made an effort to stay awake till they returned. He smiled.

'Hi, Dad.'

It was the first time he'd called him that. Rick couldn't analyse the odd squeeze in his chest. Didn't want to, anyway.

'Hi, buddy.'

It was Sarah's turn next.

'Can I call you Mum?' Josh asked.

Sarah's smile was poignant. 'Sure, hon. If you want to.'

'I do.' Josh let his eyes drift shut. 'I want to have a mum and a dad cos it's cool. And when I get out of hospital we can all live together.'

Rick felt his blood draining away from anywhere particularly useful. He felt suddenly chilled. He couldn't think even.

There was a moment's loaded silence and then Josh's eyes snapped open.

'With Harry,' he added firmly.

And that was that. Within seconds, he was asleep. Sarah fussed with his pillows and blankets. She didn't seem to know what to say and no wonder. Rick sure as hell couldn't think of anything. His mouth felt dry.

'I…um…guess I'll see you tomorrow.'

'Sure.'

Sarah glanced up and Rick knew she would be smiling but his gaze involuntarily averted itself so fast he couldn't be sure. He knew he should say something. Make sure that he and Sarah were on the same page and that they would be able to come up with some explanation for Josh as to why the happy-family thing wouldn't be happening. Laugh it off maybe and everything would feel right again.

But the words just didn't seem to be available. Or rather there were too many of them. Loud words, crowding his head. Making him feel trapped.

He had to escape.

'Chill? How can I, Max? Josh thinks we're all going to live together. That I'm going to sell my place and find something with a picket fence and be there every day to help him throw sticks for his dog.'

'He's a little boy, Rick. He's got a wish list with what every kid wants at the top of it. A family.'

'I'm *not* a family man. You know that.'

'Do I?' The voice on the other end of the line sounded thoughtful. 'I know you didn't think you were but things change, you know? It's not as bad as you think, mate. In fact, I have to say, it's got its advantages.'

Rick closed his eyes, shutting out the lights of the wharf. He hadn't been home for that long but the sanctuary of his bachelor's pad didn't hold any of its customary magic. He let his head sink onto the back of the couch and used his free hand to rub his forehead. Max was being no help at all here. He should have expected that. His friend was newly married, with a family home and a baby. There might not be a picket fence around that hillside property on the other side of the harbour but he was happily hemmed in by what it represented.

'Rick? You still there?'

'Yeah…'

'Don't get freaked out. He's just a kid. They say stuff.'

'Sarah could have said something. *Hell*, maybe she *did* say something. Maybe that's why he's thinking like that.'

'I'm sure she didn't but it makes no difference anyway.' Max sounded serious. 'The pace is your choice. You've had some big stuff to get used to in a very short space of time.' His voice lightened. 'It might not have been the best idea to jump Sarah so soon but, hey, I can totally see why it happened. You guys are perfect for each other.'

'We're just seeing each other, that's *all*. Having fun. Nobody's supposed to get hurt, including Josh. *Especially* Josh.' Rick groaned. 'I put my hand up to help. I was happy to be a donor. I even quite like being a part-time dad but if I'd seen this coming, I could have stayed a million miles away.'

There was a moment's silence before Max spoke quietly.

'Would you?'

Rick said nothing. That confusing mix of guilt and desire he'd felt before this thing had started between himself and Sarah had nothing on how he was feeling right now. His life was a mess. He couldn't even think where to start trying to unravel it all.

Into this silence came the bleep of his mobile phone.

'Got to go, mate,' he told Max. 'I texted Jet to call me when he had a moment and that's probably him.'

'No worries. Talk to you later. Just…hang in there, OK? It'll sort itself.'

'Yeah…sure.' Rick ended the call on his landline and picked up his mobile. 'Jet…Hey!'

'Hey, man. I've got precisely two minutes. There's a pilot about to start tapping his foot out on the runway. What's up?'

No pressure here. Any hope of finding a starting point evaporated. It would sound silly to say that his son had acquired a dog but wasn't that what had started this? He wanted a place to live with Harry. Parents to go along with the house. A twenty-four-seven family. The spiral of thoughts was getting faster. Too quick to catch. Much easier to shove it all into that 'too hard' basket.

'What's up with you? Where are you flying off to?'

'Haven't you heard? There's an island exploding. What planet have you been on for the last few hours, man?'

One that he'd really, really like to get off. 'Tell me.'

'Major earthquake on this island north of New Zealand somewhere. There's a team of people from the Department of Conservation there and there's been major injuries from the 'quake. It's kind of urgent to evacuate them because this island happens to be an active volcano and the 'quake seems to be a pre-eruption warning.' Jet was talking very fast. This was clearly an exciting mission. 'There's nowhere to land a plane and any ships are too far away to be helpful. We've got choppers deployed in other places so they're calling in a civilian Medevac bird. I'm flying into Auckland to collect it. Should be first on the scene.'

'Wow.' This certainly wasn't the time to be asking Jet for advice on how to manage the insignificant problem of how to deal with an exploding relationship. He knew what he'd say anyway.

Cut loose, man. Plenty more fish in the sea.

And maybe he didn't actually want to hear that despite having rung for precisely that advice. There weren't plenty more like Sarah out there.

Or Josh, for that matter.

This wasn't helping any more than talking to Max. His mates were at opposite ends of the spectrum and Rick didn't want to climb onto that seesaw to find himself sliding up and down, completely out of control. His head was quite messed up enough already, thanks very much.

'Good luck,' was all he said. 'Enjoy.'

'I intend to.' Jet's chuckle was carefree. 'Talk soon.'

The beeping on his phone told him that Jet had hung up. Rick dropped it onto the couch beside him and closed his eyes again. Silence settled around him, as heavy as his heart.

Happiness and misery.

Two sides of a coin that could get flipped. Just like that.

Sarah had seen the expression on Rick's face when Josh had been dreaming out loud in an uncanny echo of her own fantasy.

Nobody could have missed the way his face had gone pale. How he couldn't get away fast enough.

From Josh.

From her.

From any notion of a shared future.

And then, as if things weren't bad enough already, Josh had woken an hour or two later. Sarah had scrubbed the tears from her face to find him running a temperature. Another few hours and he was coughing. His oxygen saturation levels started dropping and his breathing had an ominous sound.

By morning it became alarmingly obvious that

Josh had somehow picked up an infection that was serious enough to be a match for any of the antibiotics he was already on. His consultant, Mike, had been here for some time, along with his registrar. A technician with a portable X-ray machine had come and gone. Blood and other samples had been despatched and results were expected soon. Katie had just been sent to chase up the labs.

So many people in and out of this small room but one person was still conspicuously absent. Was Rick going to deal with some new emotional obstacles by doing a repeat of his avoidance tactics? Now? When Sarah needed him there so desperately? Josh needed him here, too, even if his level of consciousness was so low he might not realise it.

Mike was listening to Josh's chest with a stethoscope. The disc looked too large against small ribs that were so prominent due to how hard it was getting for him to breathe.

'We might have to intubate him and get him

onto a ventilator,' Mike said as he straightened. 'I'm sorry, Sarah.'

She couldn't say anything. The lump in her throat was too painful to try and shift it by swallowing.

'Could you go and get Katie for me? We'll need some extra hands.'

It was good to have something to do when you felt so incredibly helpless. It wasn't far to the nurses' station where Katie was probably still on the phone, talking to lab staff.

Josh's nurse *was* talking but not on the phone. Rick was leaning against the other side of the counter and they were both smiling at whatever was being said. Sarah's steps slowed. She was shocked by how relaxed they looked. Didn't they know the world was falling apart?

She was also shocked by Rick's smile and his body language. It took her right back to when she'd seen him that very first time at the wedding. The way he'd looked at her. She'd known he'd fancied her and she'd seen that he was used to getting what he wanted from women.

Was he looking at Katie like that?

A knee-jerk reaction to the awful prospect he'd been presented with last night of having to spend the rest of his life with only one woman?

She was closer to the desk now. Katie and Rick both looked up and any lightness seemed to drain rapidly from their expressions to the point where they both looked…worried. Guilty, even?

Oh…*Lord*…

'You're needed, Katie,' Sarah managed to say. 'Mike said—'

She didn't get a chance to pass on the consultant's message. An alarm began to sound behind the counter and a red light on the wall was flashing.

'*Cardiac arrest*,' Katie gasped.

'Where's the crash cart?' Rick snapped.

'Here.' Katie was already pulling it from the corner of the station area.

'What room?'

But Katie was running. Sarah had to step aside to let her pass and Rick was following. They were running over the same route she'd just taken to get to them.

She watched them skid to a halt and her silent prayer became pointless.

The door to Josh's room was flung open.

CHAPTER TEN

SARAH could only see the backs of the doctors bent over Josh's bed when she rushed into the room.

Were they doing CPR?

'Suction.' That was Mike's voice. 'Katie, grab a bag mask, would you, please?'

The nurse was standing beside the crash cart, holding a package that Sarah knew contained paediatric patches for defibrillation. The package was dropped, unopened, as Katie pulled open a drawer beneath where the lifepack was positioned on top of the trolley.

Were the patches not needed? Was it too late or were they just going to give some respirations first, the way you had to with children?

Oh…*God*…

Sarah wrapped her arms around herself, pressing closer to the wall to stay out of everybody's way. This couldn't be the end, surely? Not like this. If she'd ever let herself think of such a dark moment, she had imagined she would be lying on the bed with Josh. Holding him in her arms.

Was it only yesterday she'd been feeling so hopeful? So damn *happy*?

Her dreams were nothing but a cloud of dust right now. If only she'd been there with him last night. How could she live with knowing that in their last hours together she'd gone away to lie in a bath, dreaming about a man? Even worse, that she'd left him with his nurse so that she could go and spend hours in bed with her lover. A man who only wanted to have fun. What had he called it?

Stress relief.

The thoughts flashed as fast as bolts of lightning in her head. Blinding and painful.

Sarah hated herself.

No. She hated Rick.

She had to move as the door opened behind her and more people tried to come into the room.

'Crash crew,' someone announced.

'Stand down.'

Mike stepped back and Sarah's breath caught as she saw Josh. Propped up on his pillows, an oxygen mask covering his face. His eyes were open. Moving. He looked terrified, until his roving gaze found Sarah. And then she could see his relief. His *need*.

With a sob, she pushed past Rick to get to the bed. Close enough to touch Josh. To make that close eye contact that had helped them both through countless, frightening incidents since this nightmare had begun.

'I'm here, hon,' she whispered fiercely. 'I'm here with you.'

The expression in his eyes was heartbreaking. She wouldn't leave his side again. Not for anything. Or anyone.

Dimly, she became aware of Mike, talking to the new arrivals who were still hovering at the door.

'Respiratory arrest…suction…cleared the obstruction.' His words became more authoritative. 'Everybody out, please. This is an isolation area.'

Rick's voice was much closer. 'He's OK, Sarah. His breathing's improved and the saturation levels have gone up with the oxygen.'

Josh was still breathing too fast, though. And his skin was hot and dry. Sarah smoothed back his hair, resting her palm on his forehead, knowing that it would feel cool for him. She looked past Rick to find Katie.

'I need a cloth,' she said. 'And a bowl of tepid water.'

Mike also had instructions for Katie. Different drugs that he wanted to add to the IV fluids. A monitoring schedule and a list of the tests that would need to be repeated. A plan had been made and was being put into action.

Josh slipped in an out of consciousness for the rest of that interminable day. People came and went, gowned and masked so that they almost blurred into one entity. Even Rick failed to stand out from the rest.

She knew he had a right to be in there, as Josh's

father, but it still didn't feel right. He had only ever wanted involvement on *his* terms. Part time. Nothing that would really disrupt his life too much.

Sarah would do anything it took to get Josh through this but she had nothing to offer except her love and the desperate, silent pleas that he would survive. She sat beside his bed and held his hand. Things happened around them but she was so focused on Josh she just let them happen. Josh was hanging on and she was there with him. Helping him.

Giving him all the strength she had in her heart.

'Did you sleep here last night?'

'Yeah…' Rick patted the arm of the reception area chair and managed a smile. 'Bit hard on the neck but it's not so bad. Katie gave me a couple of blankets.'

At least he'd had a few hours' rest. He could be pretty sure that Sarah hadn't slept a wink, even though this crisis had been going for thirty-six hours now.

Max and Ellie exchanged a glance.

'Have you persuaded her to take any kind of a break yet?'

Rick shook his head wearily. There was no point whining about Sarah not listening to anything he said. Or caring about how he might be feeling. He could understand her preoccupation with Josh, of course, but she didn't seem to understand that he was a part of all this. Or maybe she didn't want him to be now that crunch time had arrived.

Whatever. He had been shut out. Sarah was so silent. Sitting there, almost ghostlike, by that bedside. Even when she did look at him, Rick had the feeling she couldn't see *him*. He was just another staff member orbiting the unit that she and Josh had been welded into.

'I've brought her some fresh clothes and a few things she might like to eat and drink.' Ellie looked down at the bags she was holding. 'I'll go and tap on the window or something. Max?'

'I'll sit here with Rick for a bit.'

Ellie's face creased into a sympathetic smile as she looked back at Rick. 'She knows you're here,' she said quietly. 'What you're doing is important, too.'

Rick gave a single nod. Both he and Max watched her walk into the business end of the bone-marrow unit. Then he cleared his throat.

'Any news?' he queried. 'About Jet?'

Max nodded. 'Helicopter did go down. They both survived. They're trapped on the island now, though, thanks to the ash from the eruption. It'll be a day or two until a ship can get there.'

Rick smiled wryly. 'He'll be all right. He's a survivor.'

Max grinned. 'He's probably thriving on the adventure of it all. He's never happier than when his adrenaline levels are sky high, eh?'

'Yeah. He does seem to attract it, doesn't he?'

'What, adventure? Danger?'

'Excitement, anyway. Bikes, planes, dramatic emergency medicine.' Rick snorted softly. 'Women.'

Max shook his head. 'He'll get tired of bouncing around like a human ping-pong ball ones of these days.'

'When he grows up?'

'Yeah…'

Rick lapsed into silence. Was that what had done it for him? Had he grown up enough, thanks to recent events, to feel tired even thinking about a lifestyle like Jet's?

Like his used to be?

What had been so great about the freedom of being a bachelor anyway? That he could do whatever pleased him? Jump on his bike and roar off up the motorway without anyone telling him how dangerous it was? Maybe he wanted someone to care about him that much. Or was it the fact that his sexual playground would be fenced off for ever? The thrill of the chase and conquest gone?

Rick felt his lips curl in distaste. A future, even with an endless array of beautiful women to play with, was just so unappealing right now.

Relationships that were so shallow because they never got past a single dimension.

He only wanted one woman.

Sarah.

And why had he been so afraid of taking a step towards being a real father and having a family of his own? Because his had been an unhappy example? Well, he wasn't his father, was he? Knowing what *not* to do should give him a great springboard into creating something good. Something so powerful it would keep him safe for the rest of his life.

Yes. He'd grown up all right. He had wisdom. He knew exactly what he wanted. What he *needed*.

Ellie came back, looking very sombre. 'Poor Josh,' she said, her voice choked. 'And poor Sarah.'

Her gaze, as she blinked hard, included Rick amongst those needing sympathy. She hugged him. And then Max hugged Ellie. They all sat together in silence for a while. One long minute dragged into another but it seemed that it was all they *could* do.

Wait.

Everything possible that could be done for Josh was being done. The raft of drugs, support for his breathing, intense monitoring of all his vital physical functions. The invisible battle being fought was in full cry and they were simply spectators.

'Can we get you anything, Rick?' Ellie whispered.

He shook his head. There was only one thing he wanted right now and, sadly, even his best friends couldn't give it to him.

He wanted Josh to pull through this. To get better. So that he didn't lose him.

He wanted to throw that ball for Harry, dammit, and see the grin on his son's face. He wanted to take them both to that beach with the sand dunes and watch them run and play until they'd both had enough and then to go…somewhere. *Home*. With a soggy, sandy dog and a slightly sunburned small boy and have Sarah waiting for them with that look that women only had for the menfolk in their lives they loved. That tolerant 'boys will be boys' kind of look.

'You guys should go home,' he said a little while later. 'Look after Mouse. And Harry. I'll call if…if anything happens.'

Which could be tonight. How long could a small, frail body hang on under the onslaught of infection?

And why was he sitting out here, for God's sake?

'I'm going in,' Rick said, standing up. 'I need to be with my…family.'

The word had come from nowhere, the hesitation barely perceptible.

Max and Ellie understood.

Would Sarah?

Sarah couldn't feel her body.

An odd kind of numbness had crept in, due to exhaustion and sitting so still for so long. Her eyes could move normally, though, and she'd seen Rick come in and position a chair on the other side of Josh's bed. She'd seen him take hold of Josh's other hand and then he'd looked up and she'd met his gaze properly for the first time in what felt like for ever.

She found her head could still move, too, as she nodded slowly. Even her lips curled and it felt strange to be smiling, even this tiniest bit.

But this felt right. So right she overcame the numbness and stretched out her other hand over the top of the bed, towards Rick. He did the same and their hands touched, their fingers interlacing.

They became a small circle of humanity. Each adult touching Josh and connected to each other.

Sarah could feel Josh's small hand enclosed within hers and her hand within Rick's. It was so much more than simply physical awareness. Time—place, even—ceased to be relevant. The world was holding its breath, maybe pushing just a little, as something new was born.

Something that held all three of them. Sarah could almost hear the echoes of laughter and tears around them. She could feel the warmth of ultimate comfort and a bottomless well of strength.

Love.

In its purest form. Flowing from hand to hand in this precious circle. And when Sarah raised her gaze to meet Rick's it seemed to flow faster. To make everything brighter. Clearer.

Part of it hurt. Maybe it was the truth she could see in the dark gaze cradling hers. She'd wanted Rick to be more than just involved by being the donor in this journey she'd been on with Josh. She'd pushed him into getting to know his son and having an emotional investment in the outcome. Well, she'd got what she wanted, hadn't she? The love Rick had for his son and the pain he was experiencing himself was as solid as his presence in this room. And his pain was her pain.

'I'm sorry,' she whispered.

'What for?'

'I've put you through so much and it might be...' The next words died on her lips.

Don't say it, Rick's gaze commanded. *Don't even think it.*

'I'm not sorry,' his voice said. 'Never think that.'

His gentle smile nearly undid her. He really meant that. Oh…dear Lord. Sarah had to look away. To focus on Josh again. She couldn't fall apart now. She had to concentrate.

To hang on.

Rick could see exactly what Sarah was doing as she took what remaining strength she had and gave it to Josh.

It was in that precise moment that he realised how much he loved this woman.

Not that he could tell Sarah that. This wasn't the place and it certainly wasn't the time.

All he could do was try and show her that he was there for the long haul. For better or worse. By being here now. By holding her hand and trying to infuse her with some of *his* strength.

He had enough for both of them.

For *all* of them.

When Katie came in to check on Josh she worked quietly around his parents. The first few times they were sitting up and were aware of her taking Josh's temperature and making notes of everything the bedside monitors were recording.

On her visit when a new day was almost breaking, she caught her breath on entering the room. Josh lay pale and still. Sarah had her head down on one arm, her face covered, and so did Rick. When she came closer, she breathed a sigh of relief and then found herself smiling. They were all sound asleep but they were all still holding hands.

She smiled again a minute or two later. Josh's fever had broken. His breathing was a lot closer to being normal.

The crisis appeared to be over.

Everybody was exhausted.

Josh continued to improve steadily physically but he was miserable. Too weak to do anything remotely interesting. Even concentrating on watching a DVD was too much, days later.

'I hate being sick.'

'I know, hon, but you're getting better every day.'

'I'll just get sick again.'

'Maybe not.' Sarah's smile was full of genuine hope. 'Your blood count's getting heaps better. Dr Mike was pretty happy this morning, wasn't he? He says the new bone marrow is starting to work and that's why you're getting better.'

But Josh wasn't listening. He had his hands on his head and tears welled in his eyes. 'I've got no hair. I'm a freak.'

'It'll grow back.'

'No, it won't,' Josh sobbed. 'I want…I want my mum.'

Sarah's heart squeezed painfully. '*I'm* here, short stuff.'

'You're only pretending to be my mum.' Josh was in a darker place than Sarah had ever seen him. It terrified her.

'And Rick's not really my dad.'

'Yes, he is.' At least Sarah could sound completely sincere about that. He was there for Josh, a hundred per cent. The joy she had seen in his face when they had woken to find Josh was winning the battle had told her that. He loved his son.

'He just didn't get the chance to be your dad before this,' she told Josh. 'He really does love you.'

And out of all the reasons she loved Rick, this was one of the most important. It was enough for now. They had a bond through Josh that meant that his father would always be in her life. Maybe, when all this was really over, there would be a chance to be close to him again for herself, but it was Josh who needed him most for the moment so Sarah was content to have him focused only on this brave little boy.

He'd been a constant visitor these last few days. Quietly supportive. Positive. Doing everything he could think of to try and cheer Josh up. Yesterday it had been a photograph of Harry, wearing a brand-new collar. He'd brought a matching lead in and hung it over the end of Josh's bed.

'Waiting for you, buddy,' he'd said. 'For when you're ready to take Harry on his first walk.'

But Josh had barely looked at the photograph, which was now pinned beside the first picture of the dog on the corkboard. The contrast between this pristine print and the first one with its curled edges from being held too much was horribly poignant.

Josh noticed what Sarah was looking at.

'He doesn't want to live with us,' he said sadly. 'Or with Harry.' He was crying again. 'I'm too sick and…and I've got no *hair*.'

Rick turned away from the door.

They hadn't heard him open it or seen him— stopped in his tracks by the sound of his son crying. He'd been shocked enough to wait, trying desperately to think of what he could possibly do to make things better.

He needed to find the right thing this time but he couldn't think straight. He needed to be somewhere he couldn't see the bowed shoulders of the woman he loved or feel himself being torn apart by the sound of a small boy's sobs.

* * *

The shower was the best place to cry.

Even though she was only a few feet away from Josh in the *en suite* bathroom, Sarah could let herself go and Josh wouldn't know how miserable she was. She could have a good cry and then patch herself up and carry on being strong and cheerful.

She'd done it before, many times, so why did today feel so much harder? Maybe she was just too tired. Or perhaps letting go of that dream she'd had about her future was taking away too much joy. Sarah gave herself a stern talking to as she dried herself and got dressed again. She'd only postponed the dream, hadn't she? Not given up on it completely. She should be over the moon that Josh was really getting well this time. That the bone-marrow transplant had been pronounced a success. There was every chance that Josh was now on the road to complete recovery.

His hair would grow back and he'd be able to go to school and be with his friends and she'd find somewhere they could live and keep Harry. And

Rick would visit them and they'd be almost—but not quite—a family.

And that was almost—but not quite—enough.

The murmur of voices came through the door of the *en suite*. Sarah turned the handle carefully and opened it quietly. Josh didn't notice because he was staring, open-mouthed, at the visitor who sat with one hip perched on the end of his bed.

Who was it?

The adult figure in the gown had a completely bald head.

Confused, Sarah stayed where she was.

'So…what do you reckon?'

'No.' Josh shook his head firmly but he was smiling.

Smiling.

And Sarah had recognised the visitor's voice. How could she not, when that deep rumble was so familiar now? So beloved she could feel it in every cell of her body? The knowledge that Rick had shaved off his gorgeous hair, presumably to convince Josh that he wasn't a freak, undid any resolutions she'd made to present a cheerful face.

Tears were streaming down her cheeks and Sarah had to hang on to the door handle and struggle for composure.

'He wouldn't mind,' Rick was saying. 'Dog's hair grows back too, you know.'

'He'd look silly.'

'But we'd know he was still the same Harry. It wouldn't matter what other people thought. Do I look silly?'

'No-o-o.'

'He'd get a bit cold, though, so maybe you're right. We'd better not shave Harry. How 'bout Sarah?'

Josh actually giggled.

'No.' It was Rick who dismissed this new suggestion. 'I love Sarah's hair just the way it is.'

'Me too.' Josh was still staring at Rick. 'Do you love Sarah?'

There was a hesitation. A silence in which Sarah stopped crying. Stopped breathing even.

'I do.'

It was a wonder they didn't hear the ragged breath Sarah took then. Maybe they did and turned to look at her but she had closed her eyes and was hanging on to the door handle for dear life, letting a wave of pure joy course through her, body and soul.

'She's pretty special,' Rick continued. 'You're very lucky to have her for a mum, Josh.'

'She's not really my mum.'

'Isn't she? What do mums do that Sarah doesn't do?'

Josh thought about that for a few seconds. 'Nothing, I guess.'

'And she loves you to bits, doesn't she?'

Josh nodded.

'So you're lucky. If Sarah loved *me*, I'd feel like the luckiest man on earth.'

She couldn't stand here and eavesdrop a moment longer. Sarah opened her eyes to find that Rick had known she was there all along. He was watching her.

Her breath caught again, somewhere in her throat. Without his hair, he looked so different. His eyes looked bigger. Darker. He looked vulnerable.

Heroic.

Two sets of dark eyes were fixed on her and the room was so quiet. They were waiting for her to say something and there was only one thing she needed to say.

'I *do* love you, Rick.'

'He's got no hair,' Josh said happily.

'I can see that.' Which wasn't entirely true because right now Sarah could see nothing but Rick's eyes and what they were telling her.

She could see *so* much love in them. They drew her closer. She had to touch him.

'It'll grow, you know.' Josh sounded supremely confident.

It would. Like the love. Sarah was very close to Rick now but they weren't touching yet. They didn't need to. The connection in the smile and gaze they were sharing was strong enough to feel physical.

'Are you going to get married, then?' Josh asked. 'And be like a real mum and dad?'

'I hope so,' Rick said softly.

'So do I,' Sarah whispered.

'When?'

'Maybe when you're completely better,' Sarah said.

'When our hair's grown back,' Rick added.

'Can Harry come?'

'Of course. He's part of the family too.' But Rick's attention was elsewhere now. He was leaning closer, intent on kissing Sarah.

Josh made a disgusted sound. 'You can't do that in front of me,' he said. 'It's gross and I'm just a kid.'

Rick had Sarah in his arms now. She knew she was still standing on the floor but she had the oddest feeling that she was flying.

'You're *our* kid,' Rick said firmly. 'So you'll just have to get used to it, buddy.'

And then he kissed her.

* * * * *

Mills & Boon® Large Print Medical

November

December

January

Mills & Boon® Large Print Medical

February

CAREER GIRL IN THE COUNTRY	Fiona Lowe
THE DOCTOR'S REASON TO STAY	Dianne Drake
WEDDING ON THE BABY WARD	Lucy Clark
SPECIAL CARE BABY MIRACLE	Lucy Clark
THE TORTURED REBEL	Alison Roberts
DATING DR DELICIOUS	Laura Iding

March

CORT MASON – DR DELECTABLE	Carol Marinelli
SURVIVAL GUIDE TO DATING YOUR BOSS	Fiona McArthur
RETURN OF THE MAVERICK	Sue MacKay
IT STARTED WITH A PREGNANCY	Scarlet Wilson
ITALIAN DOCTOR, NO STRINGS ATTACHED	Kate Hardy
MIRACLE TIMES TWO	Josie Metcalfe

April

BREAKING HER NO-DATES RULE	Emily Forbes
WAKING UP WITH DR OFF-LIMITS	Amy Andrews
TEMPTED BY DR DAISY	Caroline Anderson
THE FIANCÉE HE CAN'T FORGET	Caroline Anderson
A COTSWOLD CHRISTMAS BRIDE	Joanna Neil
ALL SHE WANTS FOR CHRISTMAS	Annie Claydon

 *Mills & Boon® Online*

Discover more romance at
www.millsandboon.co.uk

- **FREE** online reads
- **Books** up to one month before shops
- **Browse our books** before you buy

...and much more!

For exclusive competitions and instant updates:

 Like us on **facebook.com/romancehq**

 Follow us on **twitter.com/millsandboonuk**

 Join us on **community.millsandboon.co.uk**

Visit us Online | Sign up for our FREE eNewsletter at **www.millsandboon.co.uk**

WEB/M&B/RTL4/LP